The
Price
of
Silence

THE
PRICE
OF
SILENCE

CAMILLA
TRINCHIERI

Published by

Soho Press, Inc.

853 Broadway

New York, NY 10003

Library of Congress Cataloging-in-Publication Data

Trinchieri, Camilla.

The price of silence / Camilla Trinchieri.

p. cm.

ISBN-13: 978-1-56947-458-7

ISBN-10: 1-56947-458-3

1. Woman teachers—Fiction. 2. Language teachers—Fiction

Trials (Murder)—Fiction. I. Title.

PS3553.R435P75 2007

813'.6—dc22

2006051226

10 9 8 7 6 5 4 3 2 1

"The past is the present, isn't it? It's the

future, too. We all try to lie out of that

but life won't let us."

—MARY TYRONE in Eugene O'Neill's
Long Day's Journey into Night

Prologue

Emma

At the courthouse, flanked by my husband and son, I walk the gauntlet of reporters pressing for personal details they will turn into something vile, unrecognizable.

"What happened in the past has no bearing on this case," I stop to tell them, this first day of my trial for murder. "There is no link, no inevitability."

Our lives are like anyone else's, I have to believe. A simple gathering of facts, of sad little coincidences, with no discernable pattern. Random twists of direction are all anyone can expect, twists that can turn into tragedy and overwhelm you, against which we have tried to defend ourselves by burying them in the basement of our souls, by building a wall of silence to lean on.

Tom wraps his arms around our son Josh and me as the cameras pelt us with flashes. We are a picture of togetherness, a family finally united.

"My wife is innocent," Tom says.

I stopped being innocent a long time ago.

ONE

ASSISTANT DISTRICT ATTORNEY Hector Guzman, the prosecutor in the Emma Perotti murder trial, which begins today, August 21, 2006, is a short, slim, tight-faced man in his late thirties. He approaches the jury and does a half turn to allow the defendant, fifty-three year old Emma Perotti, and her attorney a view of his profile as he makes his opening statement.

"The evidence you will hear in this courtroom during the following days will prove beyond a reasonable doubt that on April 19, 2005, Emma Perotti went to the loft that, until a few weeks before, she had shared with An-ling Huang, knocked her down, then took a can of insulation foam, stuck the plastic straw of that can of insulation foam down the throat of the unconscious girl and pressed the nozzle, suffocating her to death.

"The evidence will show that Emma Perotti had a good motive for killing An-ling Huang. The evidence will show—"

Emma

Ribbons of memory float across my line of vision, blocking out the prosecutor, the men and women in the jury, the courtroom itself:

She slipped into the morning class, my beginner's class, almost four years ago, just as Eric finished reading the chapter, "What I Miss About My Country," from the *Let's Start Reading* book.

"What do you miss, Eric?" I asked after a quick nod of acknowledgment to the new girl.

"I miss medicine." Eric folded the photocopied chapter. The classes are free for newly-arrived immigrants at the Welcome School, where I teach, and the school doesn't have money to buy enough books. "In China go direct to doctor," he said. "No call before, get medicine, take care quickly." Eric's words came out in a jumbled rush. He wouldn't slow down no matter how often I asked him to. He claimed it was because of his Chinese name, Jun. It means "a strong white horse who runs fast, ten thousand miles a day."

All my Asian students change their names—Vicki, Jennifer, John, Charlie. They say their Asian names are too hard for Americans to pronounce. I'm the granddaughter of immigrants and I often wonder if my students aren't trying to keep their two identities apart. My Italian grandmother refused to speak English, believing that the harsh-sounding words would feast on her brain and make her Italian memories disappear.

* * *

The newcomer sat next to Jennifer, my best student. They were a study in contrasts. Jennifer, from Beijing, was small, moon-faced and full of pep. She wore tight-fitting clothes, kept her short hair spiked with gel and was always offering a toothy grin lined with bright red lipstick. The new student was tall, with strong shoulders, hands that were disproportionate in their smallness and stained with paint, protruding from an equally stained, shapeless, navy-blue quilted jacket. Her hair fell thickly to her shoulders framing a triangle of a face with a wide forehead tapering down to a small pointed chin. Her hair fell thickly to her shoulders. She held her back and neck straight, as if she were balancing a heavy basket on her head. Her seriousness, her con-centration, made me think of a child faced with a difficult task.

"Welcome, I'm Emma, the teacher." I handed her a copy of the chapter we were working on. She said nothing and I held my questions until after class, when the other students would be gone. It's hard to sit in front of strangers and mouth a string of syllables that are senseless and crude compared to the music of one's own language. To commit to words that have no past, no resonance. "I am happy to have a new stu-dent," I said. Her response was a sweet, gleaming smile that made me instantly like her. "I hope you will enjoy our class."

She turned toward the large window, which overlooked a small park. On the wet windowsill three pigeons bobbed their heads, eating the popcorn Charlie, from Taipei, had put there. The day before it had snowed four inches in New York City and today the sun reflecting off the snow filled the room with a stark white light. The girl flinched. She closed her eyes.

"It's too bright in here," I said and walked over to the window.

"No!" Esmeralda, from El Salvador, protested after I pulled the shade down halfway. "Is nice. What I miss about my country is the sun."

"I miss—" The new girl stopped, opened her eyes.

"What do you miss?" I asked after a moment. She shook her head. Did she not know the meaning of the word? Or was it simply too difficult to continue?

"Let's put the chapter away for today and go over yesterday's homework." I wiped the blackboard clean. "Jennifer, why don't you read yours out loud."

Toward the end of class I set a date for the Christmas party three weeks away and asked my students to bring a dish typical of their country. "I'll bring lasagna," I said. Esmeralda announced that she preferred pizza.

"Would you like to bring something?" I asked the new girl. "The school will pay you back." The truth was the teachers chipped in. "A little something?" She looked blankly at the blackboard where I'd written down everyone's contribution. Jennifer translated in Cantonese. The girl looked down at her hands. Jennifer, always eager to show off her knowledge, tried Mandarin. The girl's head stayed down.

"That's all right," I said. "You don't have to bring anything. But please come. We'll have a good time."

She looked up, studied my face with what I took to be a curious, puzzled look. Much later she told me that she was staring at the ghost of sadness sitting on my face. I would discover that sadness was something we shared.

After class, I learned that her name was An-ling Huang. "English bad. Lady Teacher teach me." I barely understood her, her accent was so strong.

"You help me." On her face appeared a sudden raw need that filled me with tenderness. "Please."

"I'll be happy to teach you, An-ling."

She repeated her name, gently correcting my pronunciation. The music of the syllables is everything. Same syllables, different sound and the meaning changes. It took me a few tries to get it right. When I did, she rewarded me with the gleam of her smile.

She'd been in this country only three months. Her family was still in mainland China.

"You must miss them very much."

She played with the wide beaded bracelets on her wrists. "I have much . . ." Her hands pressed against her chest.

"It hurts," I said. After teaching hundreds of students, I pride myself in thinking that I understand new immigrants. They come to the States for a better life, but once here they discover that something visceral has been torn from them. A part of who they are—daughter, wife, mother, friend, neighbor—that is intricately tied to their homeland.

"I will help you as much as I can, An-ling. Did I say it right?"

She nodded with a smile.

"I'll see you tomorrow, nine o'clock." I handed her a copy of the class schedule. "Welcome to my class." A quick bob of her head and she slipped out of the room without a word.

In the days that followed, I looked up whenever the classroom door opened, expecting to see her.

• • •

Arnold Fishkin, Emma Perotti's principal defense lawyer, is a short, plump man in his fifties with boyish looks and a gentle manner that relaxes witnesses and wins him points with the jury.

"Emma Perotti loved An-ling Huang as though she was her own daughter. She took this young fragile woman under her wing, shored her up, gave her strength that she desperately needed. You will come to understand that Emma Perotti did not kill An-ling Huang. You'll come to understand that Emma Perotti is a good person, a highly regarded teacher of English as a second language, a woman who has dedicated herself to giving new immigrants the means to ease their way into this big country of ours. You will learn that Emma Perotti is a loving mother to her fifteen-year-old son, Josh, a loving wife to Tom Howell.

A cloudy August morning. It was only eight o'clock but Broadway was already filling up with parents and first-year Barnard and Columbia students. The parents were dressed formally, some with masks of tight-lipped determination on their faces, some with looks of awed sadness. One father lagged behind, calling to his daughter to notice the sailboats on the Hudson, the graffiti on the newsstand wall, clinging to his vanishing role as teacher, expert in the secrets of life. Next to him, the mother cried into a tissue. The daughter was beautiful in her youth, filled with eagerness to get on with her life. Watching her reawakened an old, numb ache and I hurried to the subway at 116th Street.

Halfway down the steps, I heard, "Lady Teacher." I turned back toward the entrance. "An-ling!" She seemed surprised that I remembered her name. Surprised and pleased. I was already late for work, but I walked back up the steps. "An-ling." I repeated. " 'Spirit of peace.' One of my students told me that's what your name means."

"Yes," she said.

We faced each other awkwardly, standing in the subway entrance like two old friends feeling guilty for not having kept in touch. People brushed past us on their way down to work, up to classes. She was wearing a faded black shirt over shapeless black pants and sneakers. Her hair spouted in a ponytail out of the back of a Yankees baseball cap. In one hand she held a large black portfolio. I found myself pleased by the thought that she was an artist, even proud. For no reason at all. "How are you?" The look of raw need was gone from her face, replaced by what I took as a newfound confidence. "You look well."

She tugged at a shirttail. The same beaded bracelets clasped her wrists. Beautiful, delicate, perhaps a family heirloom.

"I'm sorry you didn't come back to class."

"I want to come back, but—" She shrugged, covered her embarrassment with a faint smile. "I find new teacher. Sorry."

Her accent was almost gone. How long had it been since she walked into my class—nine months? Then I had barely been able to understand her.

"Good for you. You're a fast learner. There's no reason to apologize."

"I am happy to see you, Lady Teacher."

She had slipped from my mind, but now I was again intrigued by her. "Please call me Emma."

"Emma," she repeated tentatively.

"Come visit us in class. You'll inspire my students to work harder. Please."

An-ling shifted her weight, then turned to look down Broadway.

"I'd better go," I said. "My students are waiting. Bye. Please come visit." As I turned to go back down, An-ling gave my shoulder a squeeze. Taken aback by the intimacy of the gesture, moments passed before I twisted around. She was already crossing the street, the black portfolio slapping her long thigh, the bulging knapsack on her back making her hips look too small to sustain that weight. Her stride was wide and fast; she knew where she was going. I silently wished her all the luck she would need. I knew she would not visit the class.

On the trip downtown to the Lower East Side, I caught a few riders staring at me. Close scrutiny in a confined space is a New York City no-no, and I briefly wondered why I was getting so much attention since my looks are unremarkable, as were my clothes. I started correcting papers and tried to ignore them.

"Who' 'appen to you?" Esmeralda asked as soon as I stepped into class.

"Nothing. Why?"

"*Sanger.*" She pointed at my left shoulder.

"No," Jennifer said. "Peony blossom. Means love and good fortune."

I pulled at my blouse—a white silk one that Tom and Josh had given me for my last birthday—in order to see. I made out what did look like petals. Later, in the bathroom mirror, the petals turned out to be four fingerprints of red paint.

An accident most likely—she hadn't realized she had paint on her fingers. It was the explanation that made the most sense.

Officer William Flanagan, a twenty-two-year veteran of the police force, is a big man with a thick neck, greying red hair and a drinker's bloated face. He was the first officer to arrive at the crime scene in response to an anonymous phone call.

"Please tell the jury how you got into the building," Guzman says.

"The front door to the building was locked, so first I rang all the bells, but there's no buzzer to let people in and no one came down to open the door, so we jimmied the lock."

"And once you got upstairs to the fifth floor, what did you find?"

"The apartment door was locked too. I checked to see if it had been tampered with, but it hadn't been. We jimmied that lock too."

"Did you later dust the door for prints?"

"Yes, after we found the body."

"Did you find any prints?"

"No."

"How many apartments are there to each floor?"

"One. It's a narrow building."

"Is there a fire escape?"

"Yes, but you can only get to it from the window next to the elevator."

"You mean the window in the hallway?"

"Yes, sir."

"In other words, Officer Flanagan, if someone tried to get into the victim's apartment using the fire escape, he or she would have only gotten as far as the hallway. He or she would have still had to deal with the locked apartment door. Is that correct?"

"Yes, sir."

Guzman turns to the jury to ask his next question. "Then in order for the murderer to get into the apartment, the victim either opened the door or the murderer had a key, is that correct?"

Fishkin shoots up from his chair. "Objection, Your Honor."

In the stunning heat of an Indian summer day, I walked across the Columbia campus on my way to the Casa Italiana for a lecture. October is always a bad, restless month, during which I get the urge to change apartments, change jobs, when I wish myself in a burlap sack being spun until I lose all sense of direction and have no idea where home is. It's the month our daughter, Amy, died, sixteen years ago.

An-ling was lying, eyes closed, on the Low Library steps, propped up on her elbows, chin to the sky. She was wearing a blue Columbia T-shirt and a short red skirt. Her feet bare, small like her hands. No bracelet interrupted the sweep of skin from elbow to hand. She is so young, I thought.

I dropped down on the steps, next to her feet. Five weeks had passed since we'd seen each other at the subway entrance. "Hi, An-ling."

At the sound of my voice she sat up, hugged her legs closed. "I ruin your blouse. You are angry with me."

"No. It was an accident, wasn't it?"

"I am so sorry. So sorry." She looked stricken.

"It's all right." The strength of her regret embarrassed me and I awkwardly patted her shoulder. "Really. It was just an old blouse."

"No accident. I give you red because I like you. Red is happy news in China. A bride wears red, gifts come in red envelopes. If a letter comes without a red border, it means bad news. I paint your blouse so you remember me."

"No chance of forgetting, that's true. Are you at the School of the Arts here?"

"Yes, I want to be artist." She closed her eyes, relaxed back onto her elbows and let the sun stroke her face. It was a strong sun that would make me blister later if I stayed out for too long, a legacy from my unknown father, maybe an Irishman. My maternal side is Sicilian, at one with the sun. I needed to get up and go to the lecture on the Italian immigrant experience, but being with An-ling was a welcome distraction.

"Are you a painter?" I asked.

"For many years, before Mao, women have no history. We work hard like men but no one see us. My mother teach me I must make people always remember me. It is my duty to all my woman ancestors."

"There are many ways of being remembered."

"I paint peony blossom on your blouse. That is my way." Her expression was sweet, soft. I wondered how old she was.

Students were calling to each other. Feet bounced over the steps like so many dropped balls. It was the time between classes. The lecture would have been well underway.

I stood up, held out my hand. "Goodbye, An-ling. Be well."

She turned my hand to look at my palm. "I tell your fortune?" The movement revealed the inside of her naked wrist. The skin looked bleached where the bracelet had kept it hidden. A light purple line, thin as a blade, extended across the band of white skin. I couldn't see the other wrist, but I knew, without a doubt, that it too had a scar. A wave of pity and nausea overwhelmed me, followed by what I can only describe as intense grief.

"Your life like a mountain. High, low. Soon very high." She looked up, joyful with the good news. She didn't realize her secret was out.

"That's great, thank you." I retrieved my hand. "I have to go."

"I am sorry I paint on your blouse."

"It's okay. Good-bye now."

She bobbed her head, a pinched, sad look now on her face. "Bye, Lady Teacher."

I walked quickly down the steps and crossed the central aisle of the campus. I had the sensation that she was following me with her eyes. I turned around to wave, but she had offered her face back to the sun.

Guzman stands behind the podium placed next to the jury stand. "When you arrived at the crime scene," he asks the medical examiner, "where was the body of An-ling Huang?"

"Behind a painted screen." Doctor Malin Patashi, originally from Pakistan, is a plump, mustached man in a tight blue suit and a yellow silk tie. "She was naked, laid out on a futon, her arms crossed over her chest. Her body was covered by a sheet."

"In your expert opinion, Doctor Patashi, is that position consistent with death by suicide?"

"No."

"Why is that?"

"As I stated a few minutes ago, the young lady died of asphyxiation caused by the expansion of insulation foam in her throat, a process that takes from thirty to fifty seconds. A short time, but painful nonetheless. Under those circumstances, the victim would not have stayed motionless under a sheet with her arms crossed over her chest."

Fishkin stands up. "Objection to the use of the word 'victim.'"

"Sustained," says Judge Sanders. She turns to the witness. "Please refer to An-ling Huang by her name."

Patashi strokes his tie. "Had An-ling Huang been conscious when her air supply was cut off with insulation foam, she would have writhed and not lain motionless under a sheet."

"During your examination of Miss Huang's body in the lab, what were you able to establish about her physical condition?"

"The young lady was healthy, with good muscle tone. She had no scarring or lesions in or around her genitalia and anus, which signifies that she was not sexually molested. There was also no trace of semen in or on her body. We checked for possible pregnancy, as that could involve motive."

"What was the result?"

"She was not pregnant."

"Were you able to make a determination as to the time of death?"

"I was indeed able to. After taking into consideration body temperature, the degree of rigor mortis, also livor mortis, and the chemical changes in the eyes, I determined that the estimated time of death was between the hours of two o'clock p.m. and five o'clock p.m. of that day, April nineteenth."

"Thank you, Doctor Patashi. No further—"

• • •

The next day, after my classes were over, I came back uptown and went directly to the School of the Arts at Columbia. The painting division was on the fourth floor of Dodge Hall. I wandered through the various studios, filled with the apricot light of the setting sun. There were only a few students around, chatting, cleaning up their palettes, critiquing each other's work. A tall, reed-thin African American in a tattered bathrobe walked past me, her head bound in turquoise silk. Her likeness was painted with varying degrees of talent on the canvases perched on easels thoughout the room.

I asked a girl standing in front of a row of sinks if she knew An-ling Huang.

"I don't know everyone's name."

"She's Chinese."

She raised a ringed eyebrow. "Yeah, with that name. We've got a lot of Asian students." Above her head a large sign announced SEXUAL HARASSMENT MUST STOP!

"She's quite tall, five-foot-seven or -eight, hair to her shoulders, wide forehead, pointed chin. A lovely . . ." smile, I was going to add, but the student turned away.

"Maybe you could check with the Dean's office," the ringed eyebrow suggested as she soaped her paintbrushes. "It's one floor down."

What would I say when I got there? "Dear Dean, I am looking for one of your students. Her name is An-ling Huang and once she tried to kill herself."

I suddenly felt foolish. What if the knife had slipped while she was helping her mother in the kitchen, or she'd fallen while carrying a glass bowl? Maybe it was only a shallow cut, a teenage cry for attention now forgotten. An-ling was not my responsibility; she didn't need or want my help.

I didn't go to the Dean's office. Later, I threw the blouse away, went back to Saks to get one just like it for Tom's and Josh's sake, and put An-ling Huang out of my mind.

Arnold Fishkin approaches the podium to cross-examine the witness. He consults a notepad before speaking.

"Doctor Patashi, you told the court that An-ling Huang had a contusion on the back of her head severe enough to have knocked her unconscious, which, in your opinion, allowed someone to insert the insulation can tube into Miss Huang's throat without a struggle, is that right?"

"That is what I told the court."

"And it is your opinion that the contusion was caused by someone hitting Miss Huang's head hard against the floor?"

"That is my opinion."

"I ask you if it is possible, in your expert opinion, that the contusion found on the back of Miss Huang's head was the result of her falling backward on her own? Slipping on something, for instance, or suddenly fainting."

"That seems *highly* unlikely. The victim was in good health, and—"

"I am asking if it is possible,"—Fishkin pauses—"possible that Miss Huang fell and hit the back of her head on her own."

Patashi looks down at his lap. "Possible."

Judge Sanders leans toward the witness. "Please speak up. The jury has to hear you."

Patashi raises his head. "It is possible."

"Is it not also possible that Miss Huang inserted the tube in her own throat and then pressed the nozzle because she wanted to end her life?"

Patashi's face seizes with indignation. "I have seen many suicides in my career. Two hundred, three hundred, maybe more. Never has anyone killed himself in such a way!"

"Is there any physical reason which would have prevented Miss Huang from killing herself in just that way?"

The witness sighs. "No."

"One more point." Fishkin glances at the notebook in his hand. "Could An-ling Huang have been laid out on the futon in the manner you found her after her death? Before rigor mortis set in?"

Patashi looks puzzled. "Of course, that is clearly what happened."

"How quickly after death does rigor mortis usually set in?"

"Much has to be taken into consideration. Air temperature, humidity, the victim's weight, how active she was before death."

"Give me an approximation. Thirty minutes? An hour?"

"Not so quickly. It begins after four hours. That is an approximation. Four hours is safe to say."

"Four hours. That's a long time." Fishkin takes time to rearrange his notes on the podium, then addresses the witness again. "Wouldn't you agree, Doctor Patashi, that between An-ling Huang's death and the setting in of rigor mortis there were four hours—no, let's be conservative and say three hours in which the defendant could go to An-ling Huang's loft and find her friend already dead and lay her body out on the futon? Wouldn't you agree there was plenty of time for that to happen?"

Patashi takes a handkerchief out of his breast pocket and wipes his face. "Yes." He refolds the handkerchief, keeps it in his hand.

"Did you, during your examination of Miss Huang's body, observe any old scars?"

"I did observe."

"How many?"

"Two."

"Please describe them to the court."

"The victim had two thin, clean, almost identical scars running across the inside of each wrist."

"What caused those scars, in your opinion?"

"They appeared to be the result of cuts inflicted either with a very sharp knife or a razorblade."

"How long ago were those scars inflicted?"

"At least three years. Maybe as long as five years."

"Could the scars be the result of an attempted suicide?"

"The scars could be."

"Can you think of any other way Miss Huang could have gotten those scars?"

Patashi looks up at Fishkin with a self-congratulatory smile. "Someone could have tried to kill her and make it look like a suicide."

Fishkin lets out a short laugh of disbelief. "Thank you. No further questions."

TWO

Tom

I HAVE, AS a teacher, as a father and husband, always preached that what we, as human beings, must strive for is the truth, that the knowledge of the truth—of cultures, religions, relationships, even mundane events—would shape us, would make up the essence of each of us.

Before I opened the door of our apartment to An-ling Huang that one evening two years ago, before that day, I went about the business of living convinced that I knew my wife after twenty-four years of marriage, that I knew my then thirteen-year-old son, that I knew myself. I have lived an illusion.

I want to say this: evidence, however damning, doesn't necessarily represent the truth.

. . .

Emma thinks we met on a movie line for *Raging Bull,* twenty-six years ago. She started talking to me because I was twirling my keys around my finger. She heard some kind of music in it. I do that when I'm mulling something over; it's an unconscious gesture. I was deciding what to do, because I'd noticed Emma looking at me—straight through me, to be more accurate. She obviously didn't recognize me. We'd met maybe a year before, at a party where we happened to be sitting next to each other on the floor, eating pasta salad. Emma had raised her fork to show me a green sliver of something.

"Pasta with pickles, can you believe?" She laughed so hard she began to choke. I slapped her back, offered her a handkerchief to wipe her eyes and we started talking. She'd just gotten a job teaching third grade at a Manhattan private school, which she was happy about, although she didn't think there was enough diversity among the students and the pay was too low. I went on too long about my dissertation, how it had become the most important concern of my life. She didn't seem to be bored.

"I admire how focused you are," she said. "I'd be scared to be that intent about anything. What if it doesn't work out? What if you lose it?"

"Then I'll rewrite."

"The only time I'm that intent is in church. God isn't going anywhere."

"Religion was the earliest mental therapy," I said, which I could see didn't win me any points.

Emma shrugged. "God is my best friend. It's what my grandmother left me, my inheritance: a love for God and

her St. Christopher medal on a chain." She stood up, handed back my handkerchief. "Thanks," she said and wove herself into the crowd in the other room.

Before leaving the party I went looking for her. I wanted
to apologize for being patronizing, but she'd already gone.

In the movie line I was trying to decide whether to say
hello and remind her we'd met or simply ignore her. Then
she spoke to me, something about the jingling keys making
her think of her parents singing. We ended up sitting
together during the movie and afterward we went out for
coffee. I didn't tell her we'd met before. I didn't want her to
remember our discussion and walk away.

We started dating, cautiously in the beginning. Emma
was quiet, guarded, a woman who didn't seem comfortable
in her skin. There were times when she would aim her dark
Italian eyes at me with an expectant expression that made
me feel that I had the answer, that I could solve the world's
problems. It made me preen like a peacock, and sometimes
made me doubt that I'd measure up. She unsettled me,
which kept me hooked.

Once I challenged her interest in me. "I want you to
know I'm an atheist," I told her, "although I do believe in
maintaining a standard of morality, behaving generously
toward others," etc., etc.

"Generosity is the most important trait in a person," she
said. "That's what a belief in God leads to, and if generosity
comes without the belief, that's your choice. I'm not trying
to convert you."

She stroked my cheek with a smile, and I felt I'd caught
the golden ring from the merry-go-round.

Sometimes, in the middle of a date, Emma would shut down. I could say anything I wanted and she'd barely respond. "Am I boring you to numbness?" I asked her once after we'd been sitting in Central Park for half an hour without saying a word.

She took my hand, held it to her face. "I'm sorry. Sometimes my emotions are so strong, they zap all my energy and I have to shut down for awhile."

"You've told me before that you only feel intensely in church."

"That's just a line. Strong emotions scare people away. They scare me."

I kissed her forehead, her nose, the hand that still held mine. "Don't be scared. Not when you're with me." That was the moment when I knew she mattered to me.

As our relationship progressed, as we started to spend our weekends together, she stopped tuning out, and I came to realize that Emma craved steadiness, the security of a routine, which she hadn't gotten growing up. Her shutdowns were dictated by fear that a change was about to take place in her life. They were her way of freezing a situation. I worked to take that fear away. I showed her that I was dependable, that life could be a steady accretion of emotional and material comforts. That is what we had in our marriage until the death of our daughter. I believe I'm not wrong in thinking that during those first years I made her happy.

While we were sitting in the coffee shop after the movie that first night, I wanted to run my fingers over her face, her hair. She had thick black hair that covered her shoulders and the most beautiful pale skin I'd ever seen. Clean like soap, smooth, sweet-smelling, reassuringly lovely.

Amy looked just like Emma.

Her death was the pivotal event. It became the hub of our lives. Our every action from that point on, even An-ling's death, radiates from that one grisly truth.

Josh

Mom loved An-ling more than she ever loved anyone else. Maybe even more than Amy.

Amy was my sister. She died before I was born. I found that out from Grams—that's my grandmother. She was Mom's mom and the only grandparent I got to know. She died too.

My parents have never talked about my sister. There are no photos of her. When I used to try to picture what my sister looked like, I'd think of Mom shrunk to baby size.

My sister was two when she died. She got run over. Grams only told me after she found out cancer was going to kill her in a year.

"Some stupid drunk asshole killed your beautiful little sister," she said. It was the first time I'd heard that word— "asshole"—and I laughed and suddenly felt like a man. I was seven and it was easier to think about the word than to think my sister would still be alive if that "asshole" didn't run over her.

Sometimes I got it into my head that my sister wasn't dead because I could feel her with me, in the silence my parents kept about her. She was just there, following me. Sometimes I'd look down at my shadow and think it was her and that any minute, she'd sink into the ground and become a deep hole at my feet. She was waiting for me to fall in and keep her company. She had to be lonely. She was dead and I was alive and I was sure she was also very angry about that. I used to think those things when I was little.

I didn't find out what really happened to Amy until Mom got arrested. It's been in all the newspapers and on TV too. Not in the trial, though. The two lawyers had a fight about it, and the judge sided with Mom's lawyer. Bringing up Amy's death in court would be "unduly prejudicial."

A lot makes sense now: Why they never told me about her. Why they have no friends. Why they never took me back to Mapleton, to the house where we lived the first two years of my life. Why Mom was always in another room in her head, even when she was standing right in front of me.

I sit behind her in the courtroom, to the side so she can tell I'm here without having to turn all the way around. I watch her chest move as she breathes. It feels unreal, like I'm in an episode of *Law and Order*. I keep thinking that Sam Waterston is going to stand up and smash the prosecutor's case to pieces.

I want out of here, back to my basement room, just hitting the drums, or playing with Max on the guitar and Ben on his electronic keyboard. We call ourselves the 3Strikes, our lame tribute to the Strokes.

Fishkin doesn't look anything like Waterston, but he said he was going to get Mom off. He promised.

* * *

Jim Craig, fingerprint expert, readjusts the glasses on his nose. He is a tall, skinny sixty-year-old man with deep dark pockets under his eyes.

"Did you find any fingerprints on the murder weapon?" Guzman asks.

"No, sir. The can was wiped clean."

"Did you find fingerprints in the rest of the apartment?"

"We found only a few partials on the bathroom window and the cabinet below the sink in the kitchenette."

"No other fingerprints?"

"No."

"In your experience, is finding so few fingerprints unusual?"

"Very. It's obvious the murderer tried to wipe the apartment clean, too."

Fishkin stands up. "Objection!"

"Sustained," Judge Sanders says. "Just answer the question, Officer, without offering opinions."

"The fingerprints you did find, who did they belong to?"

"Some to An-ling Huang."

"And the other fingerprints, were you able to establish who they belonged to?"

"Yes sir. They belonged to the defendant."

Emma

I took walks around the Columbia campus after my classes. I was tired most days and told myself the walk was a way to lay aside thoughts of work, to catch my breath before going home. Amy had folded herself into my thoughts again. Morning was the worst time. I'd wake up with the feeling of her soft weight curling into me, her neck, hot with sleep, on my arm. Contentment would spread under my skin, and for a few moments, I'd breathe in unison with my daughter once again. Then a sound—the shower being turned on, a door being opened, Tom's electric razor—and Amy would be gone. I'd turn to the bedroom window and see that it faced a wall. I was in Manhattan, not in Mapleton with Amy. I would close my eyes and pretend to be asleep, hoping my face betrayed nothing to Tom.

I held Amy in the ambulance, carried her into the hospital, embraced her until a nurse pried her from my arms. No one stopped my screams.

I would lie on the floor of Amy's room at night, running the reel—hopelessly short—of Amy's life in my head, sometimes ending up asleep, more often not. I can't remember for how long this continued.

During Christmas break, my walks around the deserted campus grew longer. Everyone had gone home to family, friends, to Vermont, the Caribbean. I sat on the steps of the library and smoked a rare cigarette, yearning for what, I didn't know. Something out of reach, beyond the range of my vision.

Along Riverside Drive, the Hudson had turned into a long slab of concrete. New Jersey was walled in by heavy mist. Christmastime makes me gag. In the apartment, I tossed the mail on the kitchen table and went to the study to input a new lesson plan on my laptop—a collection of words and sentences culled from hip magazines with which

I hoped to snare my new class. On an impulse I called Tom at his office.

"Did it happen?" I asked. Tom had been waiting to hear whether he'd be the new chairman of the Economics Department.

"No," he said, then asked me to check the refrigerator. "We're running out of orange juice." He sounded busy, unfazed by the news, even though he had coveted the position for the past six years. This was the third time he'd not been chosen.

"Let's go out," I offered. "Dinner at the Terrace." It's the only really fancy restaurant in our neighborhood. Familiar, comfortable, expensive, where we celebrate birthdays and wedding anniversaries.

"I'm working late."

"We'll wait."

"I'll tell Josh about the chairmanship."

"Of course." But I was sure he would tell him nothing and Josh wouldn't ask. We live in a realm of silence.

"I'll make a dinner reservation for nine o'clock." I hung up the phone and went to the basement, following the trail of Josh's drum beats along the narrow corridor. Sometimes they are so ferocious, you can hear them pulsing through the turn-of-the-century marble of the lobby. The small rooms in the basement had, in another era, been maid's rooms. Now most apartment owners used them for storage.

I knocked. How could he possibly hear me above his battering? He used to sit on the kitchen floor, two years old, banging on the table leg with whatever object he could get hold of, his face shining with joy.

I tried the door—for once it was unlocked—opened it just enough to stick my head through and wave an arm to get Josh's attention. When he looked up, his expression was dazed. I'd awakened him from the deep of his music.

"Sorry, Josh. I did knock. We're going out to dinner, the three of us."

"Can't."

"Why not?"

"Max and me have to study for a chem test." His eyes turned back to his beloved drum set.

"Max and I," I corrected, suspecting that he preferred studying to a two-hour meal in dress-up clothes.

"There's nothing to eat in the fridge, Mom."

"I'll leave money for takeout. We'll miss you." I closed the door. Josh started up again. Drum beats were Josh's words and I didn't pretend to understand them.

Upstairs, I opened the refrigerator. The guys were right: empty. I told myself that my husband and son were perfectly capable of buying their own food and slammed the door shut. Then I thought, Josh is just thirteen and Tom was not picked as chairman, and my little outburst felt selfish.

I made the reservation and asked for a table by the window, with its northern view of the city, a stunning display. Then I went out to buy orange juice and some food at a grocery store on Broadway. I picked up frozen creamed spinach, buttered French beans, and wondered if it was Tom's intensity, his rigidity, that kept his colleagues from voting for him. They didn't know what life had dealt him, but they might have sensed his anger. Some students complained that he was harsh, that he expected too much. Most revered him.

At the checkout counter, I heard the rumble of a train beneath my feet and on an impulse, with the shopping bag digging into my arm, I rode the subway to Macy's.

At the restaurant, with the reflection of multicolored Christmas lights blending with the lights of Harlem and in the distance the George Washington Bridge. Tom opened my "Top Dog" present. He eyed the sweater, thanked me, kissed my cheek. "Feel it," I urged him. I wanted him to recognize its softness, to know it was made of cashmere. Expensive, special.

He shook it out of the box, held it up under his face, imitating my way of checking out a new item of clothing. "You won't lose me in a crowd with this." He was teasing me, but I realized that the color, a fire-engine red, was wrong. Tom likes discreet colors. Heather green is his favorite.

"I'm sorry; it's too loud. I'll exchange it. I don't know what I was thinking." Red for happiness, An-ling had said.

"Give it to Josh," Tom suggested. "He could use some grown-up attire."

"No. It's for you." I took the box from him. "I'll exchange it." I touched his fingers coiled around the wine glass. "I'm sorry, Tom."

He raised his glass, took a small sip. I looked at my empty hand on the tablecloth, retracted it to my lap. "It's fine, Emma. I'll have more time to write. There's an article I've been working on that may turn out to be the first chapter of a new book."

"What about?"

"The impact of terrorism on the buying patterns of the American public. Stop looking at me in that maudlin way. As Josh might put it, getting turned down for chairman is 'no big deal.' " We both knew he was lying.

We ate in silence. I ended up drinking most of the wine. As the alcohol took effect, I wondered why he had married me, why I had let him. There he was in the movie line, jingling his keys, instantly familiar, like the guy who's been living next door all your life, the kindred soul my grandmother used to talk about—a gift you would receive from God if you were good enough, devout enough. He's the one, I had thought, making music so that I can hear him. It was nonsense and yet I had wanted to believe, as I had wanted to believe in Lazarus rising from the dead and the loaves and fishes multiplying. Let it be, this story of twin souls, let sweetness and love be.

That resolve would come and go the first year of our relationship. I could see the puzzled look on Tom's face when I retreated from him. A test, maybe, to see if he would come back. He did. Always. He was constant, loyal. He cared deeply. That was why I married him, why I loved him. So much has changed in our lives, but I still love him.

"I depend on you," I said as we finished our desserts.

He paid the check. If he'd heard me, he didn't let on.

Back at home I eyed the living room sofa and wanted to make love on it, to play at being young and carefree, something that perhaps I've never been. I wanted to groan and roll and heave with Tom in our pristine living room, in our kitchen, anywhere but the bedroom, the only room sanctified for sex.

I ended up making love to Tom on top of the bed, undressing him, taking off my clothes on my own. I was in charge of our lovemaking for once. Tom stayed with me as I took a long time in coming, not the usual half-hearted moan that let Tom know he could stop. Afterward I groggily wondered if I was too old to get pregnant.

In the morning, lying in the empty bed with a headache, a hot flash reminded me I would never have another child.

THREE

Tom

I USED TO watch my wife and my daughter kiss each other's hands, fingertip after fingertip, two kids delighting in each other's sweetness. They were so filled with love they could not stay apart for more than an hour or two. I watched, fat with pride, and assumed that life would continue to treat us fairly. Hard work rewarded, love reciprocated, good health as long as we took care of ourselves. It was what this country was all about, what I had been led to expect.

Twenty months after we met, Emma and I got married and moved to Westchester, picking Mapleton because it had a good school system. We wanted kids right from the start. We both had careers in teaching. I had obtained an assistant professorship in the Economics Department at SUNY Purchase, a tenure-track position. Emma was a substitute teacher for a year after our move and then taught fourth grade at a private school in Armonk until Amy was born.

Emma had two miscarriages before Amy. She was still religious then. Mass every Sunday without fail, confession every week. When she got pregnant the second time, she began praying every night on her knees in front of the bed like a little kid, going to Mass in the morning before school, lighting candles to the Madonna and St. Francis. After she miscarried again I think Emma would have given up sex if she had thought God would send over the Archangel Gabriel to get her pregnant. I don't mean to sound flippant. I was glad she had faith to comfort her. When she got pregnant with Amy she made vows. No movies for six months. She gave up restaurants, pasta and chocolate. She wanted me to abstain too, afraid her resolve would break down. On class days, at lunchtime sometimes I'd drive over to our favorite restaurant in Silver Lake, and gorge myself on spaghetti and meatballs. I brushed my teeth before going home.

We held our breaths through the dreaded first trimester. It passed without incident and we spread the good news, bought too many toys and baby clothes. We turned the study into a baby room. I scraped the old paint off the walls, papered them with green stripes, added the rabbit border on which Emma had set her heart.

While I shaved in the morning she'd sit on the lid of the toilet, an ecstatic expression on her face, and prattle on about the delicious visions her raging hormones had released during the night. Her eyes, her skin glowed. It is possible to shine with happiness. I saw it with my own eyes. The only dream of hers I remember was of her surrounded by baskets filled with babies as tiny as chicks. The babies kept multiplying and Emma kept turning the baskets over and spilling the babies over herself until she disappeared underneath them.

Two months before the due date, Emma's placenta started peeling from the wall of her uterus, a condition that confined her to bed, where she fought hard to keep calm, breathing in and out with a steady rhythm that tired her and kept her from hysteria.

Luckily, I was only teaching two classes then and had plenty of time to take care of her.

Emma asked me to go to Mass in her stead to pray that the baby would be safe, and I went, believing none of it. But when Amy was born, a healthy seven-pound baby, I filled the church with flowers.

Becoming a father was a powerfully altering experience. Amy's presence in our lives left us dazzled. In Emma's view we'd been pulled out of a deep hole in the ground and radiated with sunlight. We were blinded by it.

As Amy grew, as she touched, explored, learned to walk, talk—normal things that babies do, I suppose, but to us they were miraculous—she became a guiding light, a constant beam in our lives. Everything else—work, sex, our love for each other—diminished in importance, became background to Amy. We had almost lost her, but she had fought to be born, and when I held her in my arms or watched her suck from Emma's breast, we assumed the battle was over, that she would be with us for the rest of our lives. That assumption made us cocky, made us careless.

At her funeral, Emma's priest said, "Thank God for giving you the joy of Amy, even if only for a short while." I was filled with too much anger to respond, but with time I came to accept that Father Caputi was right. Not to have known Amy is inconceivable to me.

There was no reaching Emma. After Amy's death, she crawled into a mental room and locked herself inside. She refused to see Father Caputi or our friends and never, to my knowledge, did she set foot in a church again. I suggested that we go to a grief therapist, but she wouldn't have it.

The department allowed me to take the rest of the semester off. I hired a woman to come over a couple of hours a day and stay with Emma so that I could drive to other towns in Westchester, park the car in some cul-de-sac and run for ten, twelve miles, on roads where no one knew me, where my anger and grief could pour off my body with my sweat. Then it was back home to hours of never letting my guard down, listening for every sound in case she called out to me, in case she asked for help. At night Emma slept on the floor of Amy's bedroom. I slept in an armchair I dragged into the hallway outside the open door. "Slept" is an exaggeration in this case. I caught naps off and on, despite the cramp in my stomach. Later, when Emma took up living again, I realized I'd been on a suicide watch—the cramp was plain and simple fear. But at the time, I couldn't see it. I thought I was simply trying to be there for her, to show her I still loved her.

I tried to help Emma with all my heart. I've thought about it a great deal and I know I didn't come up short. I bought her books on grief, took her out for rides, rented movies she never watched, tried to get her to talk, cry. I did the best I could. It's useless to ask for more from a person. Each of us comes equipped with a given capacity for generosity, for love, caring, patience, even for grief. Genes, experience, parents, whatever, determine that by a certain time—your teens, your twenties—there it is, a jugful of emotions, a specific quantity. There's no refilling. Once the quantity gets used up, there's no more.

Emma

I was driving home, to Tom and Amy. In the back seat was a big stuffed dog, a Lab, bought to appease Amy for the puppy she kept crying for, that I couldn't give her because of my allergies. The afternoon shone, as if wiped clean with Windex. The leaves on the trees had turned and pumpkins grinned on the front steps next to wooden vats of chrysanthemums. It was a cinematic day, precious in its prettiness.

I turned the sharp corner onto Longmeadow Road and relaxed my grip on the steering wheel. Home was an easy mile and a half away. I revved the Buick up to fifty miles an hour in a thirty-five-mile-an-hour speed zone. There were never any police on this stretch of the road and I was eager to get back.

At the turnoff to my street, my neighbor's golden retriever stood on the corner, wagging her tail at me, her milk-filled teats swaying rhythmically. A dog as dumb as she was sweet, she was always running off. I swung into my street. Our home was four houses down, on the right, a small white two-story with a short front lawn edged with rhododendrons that needed pruning. I'll get to it tomorrow, I promised myself. The dog barked, her tail now whipping the air.

"Go home, Sandy!" I called out.

The dog lifted her head, ears cocked.

"Home!"

She streaked in front of my car. I jerked the steering wheel to the right, away from her. The car skidded. Out of the corner of my eye I caught colors shifting low on the sidewalk, a darting movement I had no time to comprehend. A yelp was followed by a soft thud. The right front tire lifted, then dropped back on the road. Then the back tire lifted and dropped back.

Up and then down.

I hit Sandy; Sandy is dead!

I cried out, yelled, as I tried to regain control of the car. A dog barked.

From the sidewalk across from where I had first seen her, Sandy wagged her tail. The surprise lifted my hands off the steering wheel.

The car kept moving for another thirty-seven feet, according to the police report. It was stopped by the fifty-year-old maple, the tree that had made Tom and I fall in love with our property. The report stated that I walked away from the accident shaken, but unharmed. Amy died in the ambulance.

Tom

One night in March, six months after Amy's death, with pellets of rain hitting the windows, I sat at my usual post in the hallway, on my fourth Scotch. Emma was lying in a tight curl on the floor of Amy's room, her nightgown bunched up high, showing the whiteness of her thighs, her face covered by her thick, glorious hair. Watching her sleep, I felt rage surge in my blood faster than the Scotch and I heaved myself out of the armchair.

"Emma." I stood in the doorway. "Emma, look at me."

She didn't respond.

"Emma, please."

I walked into the room, knelt down. "Emma. Answer me." I reached over and shook her shoulder. She cringed at my touch with a protesting whimper.

"Damn it, Emma, stop shutting me out. You're going to sleep in your bed tonight, next to your husband, the father of our dead child. You hear me? *Our* child, Emma!" I pulled her to me to lift her up, carry her back to our room. She recoiled, grew rigid, rolled herself out of reach. Since Amy's death she hadn't let me hold her or touch her. Not in the hospital waiting for Amy's body to be released. Not at the funeral. Not once in six months. I lay on the floor next to her, pulled her to me. She went limp. The sudden feel of her, soft and warm against my chest, my groin, started me crying.

"You're not the only one suffering. I loved Amy just as much as you did. I love you. I need your help. I want to help you. Please Emma, let me in."

Emma said nothing. Her only movement was a breath that tickled my arm. I could have cried, cajoled all night long. It would have made no difference. I was nothing to her.

"God damn it, I'm your husband." I hiked up her night-gown. She kicked me and struggled against my chest. I cupped her breast; my arm pinned her down. My free hand rubbed between her thighs. She bucked, wriggled, kicked. Not a sound came out of her mouth. The more she fought me the greater my anger and my desire to have her became until I turned myself over on top of her and raped my wife.

It was the worst thing I could have done to Emma and I am still deeply ashamed. At first I deluded myself into thinking that all I had wanted from her was some kind of recognition that I was still in her life, that our marriage mattered, but the truth is not as kind. I wanted to hurt her because I blamed her for Amy's death.

The coroner's report said that Amy's death was an accident. The police pressed no charges. A tragic accident, the neighbors, our friends, agreed. Blame is useless, Father Caputi said, but that didn't stop me from blaming Emma.

I woke up on the floor of my daughter's room, with the stink of Scotch and sweat all over me. Emma was standing above me, fully dressed for the first time since the funeral, with a cup of coffee in her hand. "I'm sorry," I said.

"I envy you your anger, Tom. Anger is palpable. You can scream it, strike with it, feel it pulsing though you. Anger is alive. Grief is like death. It's a fog slipping through you. It smothers your heart."

She never considered that my anger was grief too.

We made love almost every night after that. Thrashing, noisy, desperate love. Animals is what we were; we came, and then we cried for Amy and for ourselves.

"We were in the Garden of Eden," Emma said. "I ate the apple."

Sitting in this courtroom, listening to the prosecution build a case against my wife, I realize I still blame her. That is my coward's truth.

FOUR

AFTER GEORGE WAGMAN states his credentials as a crime scene investigator, Guzman asks him if he examined the sheets and pillowcase found on the victim's futon.

"I did." Wagman, a tall, wide-shouldered African American in his mid-thirties slouches over the railing of the witness box.

"What did you find?"

"Seven strands of the victim's hair."

"Is that all you found?"

"I found soap powder."

"Nothing else?"

"Traces of body oil, makeup on the pillowcase. The sheets and pillowcases were washed that day."

"How can you tell?"

"I could smell the softener. And the inside of the dryer was still warm."

"Did you examine the towels?"

"I sure did. Same soap powder, same softener smell." Wagman turns and smiles at the jury. "My wife uses that stuff."

"Did you find soap powder or smell the softener on any other items in the loft? Her clothing, for instance."

"No, just the towels in the bathroom and the sheets and pillowcase on the futon."

"Is that behavior, washing the sheets and the towels, consistent with someone trying to cover her tracks?"

Fishkin stands up, waving his arms in exasperation. "Objection!"

"Overruled. You may answer the question."

"Sure is consistent," Wagman says, "if the 'someone' has any sense. Not all of them do, you know."

"In your extensive search of Miss Huang's loft, did you find a laptop?"

"No."

"Did you find a gold St. Christopher medal on a chain?"

Wagman shakes his head. "No medal and no chain."

Emma

Scrunched between bodies in the KGB Bar in the East Village, I listened to a colleague reading his poems, just published by a small press. Lenny, a thick-set man in his forties, rocked back and forth in the far corner of the bar, his words sharp rhythmic jabs at the microphone. His expression was ferocious, and I was caught, unaware, by a memory of one of my mother's lovers, standing on the coffee table in the living room, spitting out Allen Ginsberg. That reading had led to loud lovemaking on the other side of her bedroom wall. Ginsberg followed by rowdy sex. At the KGB it seemed a natural sequence. When I was six years old, it turned my stomach.

During a break in the reading, a young woman urged us to order more drinks. I elbowed my way to the bar and asked for a Pellegrino.

Next to me, a man said, "I find poetry incomprehensible." He was tanned, silver-haired, somewhere in his fifties and arrogantly handsome. I was ready to ignore him, but he introduced himself.

"Doctor Robert Feldman, plastic surgeon." As he spoke he studied the map of wrinkles on my face. I didn't need him to tell me I was the oldest woman in this crowd of fans and literary hopefuls.

"Why did you come then?" I asked, without giving my name.

"I was coerced by a friend of yours." He turned and wrapped an arm around An-ling's waist, bringing her forward.

"Hello, An-ling." My voice betrayed my surprise.

She wore a jade-green silk Chinese dress with a high collar and slits running up her thighs. Her hair fell loose over her shoulders and her face was gaudy with makeup. The beaded bracelets were back on her wrists.

"I am happy I find you." An-ling slid out of the doctor's grasp and walked over to the door, where there was more breathing space. I followed.

"How did you know I'd be here?" I asked.

"I go to the school this afternoon to find you. You are not there, but a big paper hangs on your door. You want students to come to KGB tonight. I am almost your student and I come."

"I'm glad you did," I whispered, "but the poster was Lenny's doing, not mine." I nodded toward the corner where Lenny had started reading again. "He's also a teacher." We moved into the stairwell so that we could keep talking. "Are you thinking of coming back to the school?"

"No." An-ling handed me her glass. I took it with a sense of déjà vu, of being the recipient of repeated gestures, small in content but large in the language of trust.

"You look different," I said. An inane statement. I held the glass to my chest and watched An-ling lift her hair, knot it in a tight bun at the nape of her neck. The crown of her head moved into the beam of the overhead light, smooth as a scrap of black satin. Why was she looking for me? "You look older."

Apart from the makeup, all the lines of her face were stronger, her expression richer. She reminded me of a Matisse woman, outlined in black. How long had it been since I'd last seen her? October to February. Four months.

"You remember me different, you know why?" She took her glass back.

Because of sex, I thought. An-ling had had a lot of sex since October. "I haven't seen you in a while."

"Tonight I am happy. That is why I look different."

"What are you happy about?"

"I am here." An-ling finished her drink, sucked on the ice. "My ancestors lived in North China, noble China. Then the Mongols come and killed many of us. We run away to the South. I was born in Su-kai, small village in district of Xin-Hui. Not a happy place."

"Where did you learn to speak English so quickly and so well?"

"Feldy says best way to learn language is to find boyfriend."

"The best way to learn *a* language is to find *a* boyfriend. You mustn't forget the articles." I adopted my clipped teacher's voice to hide my anger at the thought of her having sex with "Feldy," so much older than she was, so obviously taking advantage of her. "How old are you?"

"To be Chinese is to be old always." She giggled. "Twenty in Chinese years, nineteen in yours. You how old?"

I stroked my neck, which, I joke to Tom, looks like an unmade bed. "Hormone-replacement old."

"No need for facelift yet." An-ling's face was mock serious.

"Well, that's a relief."

"Feldy" appeared in the doorway. "There you are."

An-ling wiggled fingers at him.

I looked at my watch. "I have to go now." Tomorrow, at school, Lenny would get my apologies.

"Where?" An-ling asked, following me downstairs to the bulging coat rack.

"Westside. Uptown."

"Are you taking taxi? I go with you?"

I'd planned on the subway. "What about Doctor Feldman?"

"He do not own me."

Outside, the temperature was in the teens, the subway four blocks away. A cab would be expensive, but warm.

"I'll drop you off," I said.

An-ling said she lived near me. I didn't stop to think how she knew where I lived. "Where exactly? The cab will drop you off first. It's much too cold to walk even a couple of blocks."

She shook her head. I wondered if it was the doctor's home she was going back to, if she didn't want me to know.

The cab swung onto the West Side Highway. Light from the streetlamps flashed across An-ling's face, animating it. In the semi-darkness of the cab she had turned from a Matisse woman to a kid trying to look sexy in her mother's clothes and makeup. How could she look so different in the space of a few minutes?

"What is your husband's name?" she asked. "Your children, you have many?" She was filled with curiosity. Where did Josh go to school? Did we have uncles and aunts, parents, grandparents? Where did I come from?

"I was born in Boston. Then my mother and I moved to the Bronx to live with my grandmother."

An-ling moved closer, eager for more. "Your mama, what is she like?" She must have caught my hesitation. "Family important to know a person. You tell me, please."

"She was a good woman." An unhappy mother who never forgave me for being born.

"And your baba?"

"My father? He died when I was little." The truth is that I have no idea who he was or whether he is still alive. I used to picture his absence as a parched field surrounding me, where nothing grew, not even weeds. When we still lived in Boston, each time my mother brought home a man, I would examine his face for a familiar curve of the jaw, length of the nose, shape of a lip that might tell me: this is the guy; this is my father. "Mine is a reduced family. Everyone else is gone. Three people: Josh, Tom and me."

"That is reason ghost of sadness sits on your face?"

She smelled of lavender. A yoga teacher once told me that the smell of lavender alters the brain cells, relaxes you. In the cab, the smell was too sweet, cloying. I wished I'd taken the subway. The ride was going to cost more than twenty dollars.

"Why did you come looking for me, An-ling?"

She tossed her head, like a restless filly. A lock of hair came loose. "You answer me first, Lady Teacher." She tucked the loose hair behind her ear.

"I'm very tired, An-ling."

She thudded back into the dark corner of the seat. Josh used to do that, throw his body against the back of whatever he was sitting on when I refused him another helping of ice cream, a toy, the TV.

"I taught three beginner classes today."

We didn't speak until the cab turned off the highway at 96th Street. "Leave me here, please," An-ling told the driver.

"Are you sure?" I asked.

Before the cab came to a complete stop, An-ling jumped out and ran across the street against the traffic light. I paid the driver, got out and chased after her. Two blocks later I caught up with her and offered to walk her home. It was only ten o'clock, but because of the cold, there were few people on the street. "Where do you live?"

"I'll walk *you* home." Her voice was firm.

I was too out of breath to argue, so we headed uptown, shoulders tight, hands in pockets for warmth.

In front of my apartment building, An-ling dug into her backpack and pressed something soft and white into my hand. I spread it open under the entrance light: an embroidered silk blouse. "It's beautiful."

"It come from China. Made with hands, not machine." Before I could thank her she threw her arms around me. "I am sorry. Very sorry. Please do not be angry with me."

I swayed in the middle of the sidewalk, with the too-sweet smell of lavender in my nose, and this strange girl's warmth pressed against me. Inside me, a knot came untied.

The next morning I riffled through the borough phone-books at school. She wasn't in any of them. Information had no listing either. I tried to picture where she lived: a small bare room in Chinatown that she rented from a family. She had a cot, a chair. Her easel was set up in front of the single window overlooking a shaft. I envisioned her painting on scrolls, gray frogs on lotus leaves, cranes, sparrows on bamboo shoots. Paintings called *guohua*, the traditional Chinese ink media, which I have seen at the Metropolitan Museum of Art. At night, before going to sleep, she would burn incense sticks and paper money for her ancestors at the altar in the corner—a custom not that different from my grandmother's nightly ritual: lighting candles to the statue of the Virgin Mary and to the pictures of her husband and parents propped on a shelf in her bedroom.

In Chinatown An-ling would be surrounded by her countrymen. Was she happy? Did she pine for her homeland? Was she thinking of her mother, who wanted her daughter to be remembered?

Or she could have lived in a one-bedroom prewar apartment in Brooklyn, shared by four girls, Caucasian, Black, Hispanic, and Chinese. They would keep each other company in their diversity. They were careless, happy-go-lucky, sex-in-the-city girls. Clothes they discarded on the floor, stacked on chairs, waiting to be fished out when needed. Pizza cartons and Chinese takeout boxes piled up in the kitchen, waiting for someone, anyone, to take them to the garbage chute. The easel lay under the bed, thick with dust motes. The pursuit of boyfriends left no time for painting.

An-ling had found a boyfriend—Doctor Feldman, plastic surgeon, who lived in a soft-carpeted duplex where An-ling had a room to herself, with a view of the trees of Central Park. When he came home, he taught her English words that, with time, became sentences, paragraphs, so many words strung into a long line so that one day she could fly on its end, like a kite in the wind.

I started laughing. I hadn't had such a silly flight of the imagination since I was in braids! I had no idea how An-ling lived or where.

I wrote a note:

"I want to invite you to my home. Please call me. I'm not a great cook, but I think you'll like my family. Be well."

I included my home and office phone numbers and, after work, I went over to Dodge Hall. This time I took the elevator to the Dean's office. Even if An-ling had dropped out, the office would have her address.

"A student's address is confidential," the young man in the front office informed me.

"I was hoping you could forward it. She was here last semester. Maybe even before that; I'm not sure." I handed over the stamped envelope, with only An-ling's name written on the front, my return address on the back.

"Sure." He answered the telephone, put the caller on hold, waved the envelope at me. "I'll check on her address and send it."

"Soon?"

"Sure." He went back to his phone call. I left. It was late and I still had to shop. Maybe I'd buy steak and make French fries. Tom and Josh loved that.

About a week later, a handwritten envelope from Columbia University arrived in the mail. Inside was my note to An-ling, still in its sealed envelope. In a separate note, someone had typed:

"No An-ling Huang on student list in the last three years."

Josh has told lies when he's wanted to simplify his life, get me or Tom off his back. Had An-ling lied about Columbia? I didn't know. A small knot of doubt about her settled in the back of my mind, where I soon forgot it.

Anton Lyubarsky arrived in New York from the Ukraine four years ago. His hair, neck, waist, and accent are all thick. He owns a hardware store in Brooklyn with three cousins.

"How far is your store from An-ling Huang's apartment?"

"Two blocks."

"Does your store stock these cans of insulation foam?" Guzman holds up what has been offered in evidence as People's Exhibit One.

"Yes." Lyubarsky nods, scratches his hands. "Yes."

The court officer hands Lyubarsky the can.

"Can you tell whether the can in your hand comes from your store?"

Lyubarsky upends the can, nods. "From my store."

"How can you be sure?"

"I write price on the bottom. Ten ninety-five. It is good price."

Guzman quickly glances over some stapled sheets of paper. "Drawing your attention to April seventeenth of last year, did you see the defendant that day?"

Lyubarsky looks at Mrs. Perotti with regret on his face. "I want to show respect. I want to do right thing. One day I want to be citizen of this country."

"Please answer the question, Mr. Lyubarsky. On April seventeenth did you see the defendant?"

"Yes."

"Where did you see her?"

"In my store."

"Can you describe what she was doing?"

"Buying."

"Can you tell the jury what exactly Mrs. Perotti bought in your store?"

"She buy can of insulation foam, but she is nice lady. She come often to store. Buy many things. She give me English grammar book. She help me."

Outside my classroom window, the small park across the street was covered with a pale green net of buds. Two dogs strained at their leashes to sniff each other. Two Hasidic women in wigs and long skirts pushed strollers in step with each other. It was our first real spring day. I opened the window, then went back to my class notes. That morning, my advanced students would work on their writing skills, on patterns of organization. I had only a few minutes before class, but I kept casting my eyes outside, to the net of buds resting on the trees, the dogs now rolling in a tangle of leashes, the Hasidic mothers on the corner, waiting for the light to change, still talking. Above them, a trail of buildings and endless sky disappearing in the distance.

I plunged my hand into my pocket, felt the scrap of paper with the number I had copied from the phonebook on it. I wasn't sure I wanted to make the call. It seemed inappropriate, invasive, dumb.

I gave up the idea when my students scattered across the classroom like diligent ants. As they found their seats I wrote on the blackboard: "When to Use Cause and Effect Order."

The students told me what they had learned from the lesson plan and I wrote:

Use to explain why an event happened.

Use to explain the results.

Use to explain what will happen because of a specific event.

I asked them to write a short essay about something that had happened to them recently, using cause and effect.

"I have a cold and I go to the doctor," offered Janna from St. Petersburg. Writing English still frightened her.

"Write it out," I told her. "Write what happened before the cold, too. One effect can have many causes. You had a cold because you were tired from studying hard and because you were tired, you overslept, making you late for class, which then made you take the subway when you normally walk. On the subway you stood in front of a sick person who sneezed in your face.

"The reverse is also true," I told the class. "One cause can have many effects. I'll let you work that one out by yourselves."

I handed out paper to the usual students who said they had forgotten to bring their notebooks. Most were sincere. A few, the ones who didn't have pencils either, I suspected needed to save their money.

I watched them write. Periodically, I sneaked glances at the window. Janna sneaked glances at her neighbor's paper and copied. She had repeated this class for three years now. She wouldn't be able to pass her GEDs this year either, but to demote her to the intermediate level would break her heart.

"Write about yourself," I whispered to her. "Don't take someone else's story. You have your own. Tell it. Two, three sentences, that's all."

What was An-ling's story?

"I'll be right back," I told the class. In my cubicle, I punched in the phone number, gave my name to the receptionist and asked to speak to Doctor Feldman.

"A consultation will cost two hundred dollars, which will be deducted from the cost of the procedure you decide upon, if you decide to proceed."

I explained that mine was a personal call, that all I wanted was a minute of his time. The doctor and I had a mutual friend, and I needed to find that friend.

"Doctor Feldman is with a patient. He has a very busy schedule." The receptionist's tone was now snippy.

"Her name is An-ling Huang." I spelled it for her. "Could you ask Doctor Feldman how I can get in touch with her, please? It's important." I spelled my name too, and left my phone number. "Remind him we met at Lenny Gershon's poetry reading at KGB."

The next morning there was a message on my voice mail from Doctor Feldman's receptionist. "Doctor Feldman knows no one by the name of An-ling Huang."

Another lie. A mixture of irritation and disappointment prompted me to make an appointment for a consultation. This time I used Tom's last name, hoping the receptionist wouldn't recognize my voice. The earliest Doctor Feldman could see me was in ten days.

Fishkin stands up, but stays behind his desk. "Mr. Lyubarsky, are there many hardware stores near you?"

"No. Good location. Next store is twenty blocks away."

"How many cans of insulation foam, on average, would you say you sell a week?"

Lyubarsky looks at Fishkin for a moment, then his eyebrows shoot up and his round face breaks into a smile. "Yes." He has understood where Fishkin is going.

"How many?" Fishkin has to repeat.

"It depends. Maybe none, maybe five." Lyubarsky's voice is loud. "Ten, if construction going on. Last year much construction. Two buildings near store. At Tercer Street and Lowry, too." Lyubarsky rocks in his chair. "My cousins and me make very good business last year."

"How many cans of insulation foam did you sell in those two months?"

"I need to look in book for number, but I know Tercer building buy one case, but in March or April I don't know. If you want, I go look and come back."

"Thank you, Mr. Lyubarsky. That won't be necessary."

FIVE

DOCTOR ROBERT FELDMAN, regarded as one of the top ten cosmetic surgeons in New York City, sits in the witness box. He is a handsome, grey-haired man, with a gym-enhanced body underneath an impeccably tailored grey suit.

"Did you know An-ling Huang?" Guzman asks.

"I did."

"For how long did you know her?"

"Five months, approximately."

"Do you know the defendant?"

"I met her twice."

"Under what circumstances?"

"The first time was at the KGB Bar during a poetry reading."

"What happened at that reading?"

"She walked off with my date."

"And who was your date?"

"An-ling Huang."

"What was your impression of their relationship that night?"

"Objection!"

"Withdrawn. When was the second time you saw the defendant."

"In my office, three weeks later."

Emma

I sat in a deep leather armchair under a canopy of spiky leaves. Two women on the other side of the waiting room flipped through magazines. Another talked on her cell phone, ordering food for a dinner party. Elegant and thin in their designer clothes, they seemed perfectly relaxed, entitled, expecting the impossible to be made possible: to be young again. Maybe I could ask Doctor Feldman to snip at my soul, tug at the grooves of my memory, smooth them out so that I could face the sunshine of the day blameless as a newborn baby, with life still ahead of me, yet to be lived.

The reason for my visit was much simpler. Possible. Finding An-ling.

The woman on the cell phone was called into the doctor's office by the receptionist. Through the opening of the door, I glimpsed a female hip, a shoulder, covered in nurse's white, a thick streak of yellow hair. Minutes passed. I read the book I had brought with me—a slim volume of prose poems by Charles Simic I had started re-reading. Years ago, the title had attracted me: *The World Does Not End*.

"Time for you," a voice said. It took me a minute to recognize her. An-ling had dyed her hair banana yellow.

"How nice!" was all I could think to say. The surprise of her being there, of her changed appearance, made me uncomfortable. I felt I'd barged in on a complete stranger. "You're working for him! I never thought of that."

"Lady Teacher." An-ling extended her arm toward the door that opened before me. I couldn't tell whether my showing up suddenly annoyed her or pleased her.

Doctor Feldman's diplomas, recognitions, and prints of bucolic scenes covered the walls of the small office. Plants rested on corner tables. The large mahogany desk was empty except for a couple of photo albums, filled with what I assumed were the before-and-after pictures of his patients.

"Sit down, please. Doctor Feldman will be with you in a few minutes," An-ling recited, then added, "Feldy," with a complicit grin.

I laughed. "I came here only because I wanted to know how to find you. Over the phone, Doctor Feldman claimed he didn't know you."

"Here I use American name. Easy to say name."

"An-ling Huang is a beautiful name and not hard to pronounce at all."

An-ling repeated her name, letting me know I'd forgotten the correct intonation.

"I'm sorry. Point well taken. I'm afraid I'm tone deaf." I held out the letter the Dean's office at Columbia had sent back. "I've been looking for you because I wanted to invite you to dinner to meet my family."

An-ling pushed the letter into the pocket of her uniform, unread.

"You must have used your American name at Columbia too," I said, relieved she hadn't lied. "What is it?"

"For you I will be An-ling." She promised to call me.

"One last question, Doctor Feldman. Where were you on April nineteenth of last year?"

"I was in St. Petersburg, delivering a lecture. Cosmetic surgery is a burgeoning business in Russia these days."

Ruffling waves of pink tied in eight, ten bundles—peonies—hiding a face. I recognized the green-flowered paper of my local Korean grocer, also the blue-quilted jacket and the paint-stained slacks.

"Welcome to my home, An-ling."

She had come without warning. More than three weeks had passed since I'd gone to Doctor Feldman's office. We were in the middle of dinner, and I asked her if she'd eaten. She lowered herself onto the chair I held out for her without answering, holding the flowers tight to her chest. The pink tips brushed her chin as her eyes scanned the kitchen, studying every detail as if she were preparing for a memory test. I was pleased to see her, moved by all those expensive peonies, and embarrassed by the paper napkins, and the food on the table, a takeout dinner that I hadn't bothered to remove from its aluminum containers.

Tom remained seated, his expression puzzled. An-ling had interrupted a sacred family routine, his daily bonding time with Josh, during which I played the role of listener. Josh hunched over his plate, continuing to shovel food down his throat. I touched his shoulder. He stopped, straightened up.

I introduced An-ling. "She's one of my new students." The lie came out before I thought it. "I invited her to dinner," I added, opening drawers, getting flatware, a napkin, a plate. I turned the radio off. I forgot to set a glass.

I added a place setting in front of An-ling and offered to take her jacket, to put the flowers in water. She stood up and extended the many bouquets to Tom with a deep bow. Later, she told me that she'd brought peonies because they are flowers of riches and honors. Twenty-five peonies—five times five, five a lucky number. An-ling wanted Tom to like her, but Tom was resistant to any intrusion in his domestic life, even one as innocuous as a dinner interruption.

An-ling's dyed hair was in stiff braids that didn't reach her shoulders and her face was clean of make-up. "Good fortune for your family," she said in a small voice, her accent deeper from shyness. "You have a beautiful home."

While I filled four vases with the flowers, Tom asked questions in a tone that wanted to convey that he was being friendly, but it was an interrogation, pure and simple.

"How long have you been in this country?" he asked.

"Seven months."

I thought that Tom must have been making her nervous because she had walked into my classroom almost a year and a half before.

"New York right away?" Tom asked.

"Before, two weeks in San Francisco."

"Why did you leave California?"

"Tom, stop. Please," I interrupted, sitting down. "Let's eat."

She did not eat. Instead, she stared at the grouping of pill containers Tom keeps in the center of the table between the salt and pepper shakers. Multivitamins, Echinacea for when he feels a cold coming on. She fingered the container of Ginkgo Biloba he'd bought the previous year after his fifty-fifth birthday.

"There is a story that tells how it happened that Ginkgo nuts are so good for you. Do you want to know?"

"Of course we do," I said.

"I tell you." She beamed.

I put down my fork and elbowed Josh to do the same. Tom kept on eating.

"A mean monk lived in a monastery where there was also a bell tower and three Ginkgo trees. Outside the monastery was a field of herbs that could cure the sick, but the mean monk will not let the poor people of the province pick the herbs. He wants them for himself and many people die. The three trees and the bell tower are angry about this and want to help the poor people. With their magic they change into three maidens and an old man and go to the field to pick the herbs. When the monk sees what they are doing, he complains to his boss, the Jade Emperor, who sends down generals to beat the maidens and the old man. The maidens see the generals, swallow the herbs, and turn themselves back into trees. From now on, the nuts of the Ginkgo trees are full of herbs that cure."

"That's a sweet fable," I said.

"China has many stories to explain many things."

"What happened to the old man?" Josh asked.

"He is only decoration. Men have too many stories."

Tom wiped his mouth, his eyes steady on An-ling. "You speak very well after such a short time. I have Asian students who have been here for many years. They have the vocabulary, but half the time I can't understand them. I should send them to you, Emma. You're obviously good."

"How about giving her the credit?" Josh pointed a fork at An-ling. "I mean, nothing against you, Mom, but she's the one who did the work."

"You're right. It is all to An-ling's credit. I did nothing." The truth of it made me laugh.

An-ling giggled and put a string bean in her mouth.

"Credit to both of you, then." Tom smiled and shot Josh a glance of parental pride. Then he reverted back to his role as inquisitor. "Do you live with your parents?"

"My parents are dead. My aunt brought me here. She lives in San Francisco."

"I'm so sorry." I stretched a hand across the table, but didn't touch her. At the school, she had only said they'd stayed behind.

"When Baba, my father, died I was two. Mama, I was twelve. I lived with Nyah-Nyah, my father's mother, until Goo-Goo Chai sent for me—that is my father's sister. I do not love my aunt. She wants to bind my brain so it will be as small as hers." An-ling punctuated the end of each sentence with a bob of her head. A smile appeared on Josh's face, like the sudden bright flash of a fish in a pond. I grasped that smile as a sign that he liked An-ling.

Tom too, I thought, let his diffidence soften, for he said, "Well, good luck to you." He fell into silence as he finished his meal. An-ling ate nothing after the one string bean. Josh cleaned his plate twice while his sneakers made little mouse sounds against the rubber tile floor. I reached below the table to steady his knee while I reiterated the beauty of her flowers, chatted about school and the students An-ling had met only once, whom she probably didn't remember. I avoided asking questions.

An-ling listened, head cocked, giving my chit-chat importance.

Tom folded his paper napkin, as always. "When exactly did you start studying with my wife?"

An-ling straightened her neck, gave me a look. I returned her gaze. Tell him if you want, I thought, as if she could read my mind. Tell him the truth. You and I barely know each other. There are no connections between us except for the red peony you painted on my blouse.

"Maybe one or two weeks after I come to New York," An-ling said.

Her complicity encouraged me. "An-ling is my best student."

Josh

All those flowers. It was over the top. She was trying to butter up Mom; that's what popped in my head then. Now I think she was scared, maybe. She wanted us to like her right away.

At first, An-ling was just someone Mom knew, one of her students. Three or four times before Mom had invited her students home for a party. They came with CDs, tapes from their countries, and they danced. It was fun. One woman tried to teach me how to samba. She wouldn't give up. I've got some beat in my arms, but I'm lousy with my feet. It was at one of those parties that I learned about Tito Puente. What a great drummer!

Last time, I couldn't find my Discman after a party and Dad was sure one of Mom's students took it. Mom got real upset with him for thinking that. I felt really bad because a few days later she found my Discman in the laundry basket. I must have thrown it in there with my sweatshirt, I guess. She never had another party.

The first time An-ling came over, Dad, right off the bat, started rapping out questions like he was Jerry Orbach. Dad doesn't know it, but he can be pretty intimidating. It didn't faze her for a second. She answered and bounced her head up and down like she was having such a good time she was going to start dancing. I tapped a counter beat with my feet. I wanted to laugh, but that wouldn't have gone over real well.

Later I found out from An-ling that the Chinese don't talk while they're eating. And when you ask questions, they don't always tell you how it is. If you ask if they're hungry, they'll say no even if they're starving. "Saving face," she said. For a while I thought being Chinese is about keeping secrets. An-ling sure had enough of them, but so did Mom and Dad. Then I started keeping some of my own.

She came over a lot after that night. I'd come home from school and she'd be in the kitchen with Mom, chopping up vegetables. An-ling wanted me to help her. "Learn how to cook, you will have many girlfriends." She asked what year I was born. I told her and she said I was born the year of the rabbit. According to her, it meant I had a lot of talent and could be trusted, which I guess is nice, but I didn't believe it.

The afternoons she was there, I'd get a Coke and go to my room or to the basement until dinnertime. I've always done that. Gone off by myself, I mean. Even when she wasn't there. I had nothing against her.

Mom thinks I'm shy. I don't get into conversations when I'm not interested, that's all. There's no point to it unless there's something really neat going on.

One time I saw Mom reading to An-ling in the park across the street from our building. Riverside Park. I stopped to listen to a guy playing Jimi Hendrix on his guitar— "Purple Haze"—what I'd just been playing in the basement.

The guitar player was really good, but Mom's voice kept covering the notes, like she had no clue she should stop making noise and just listen to the music. She went on reading from this little book she had in her hands. An-ling was sitting in front of her, facing me, both of them on an old knit blanket full of holes from me poking at it when it was on my bed when I was little. Grams gave it to me when I was born. She told me she knitted it especially for me, which I know isn't true because I overheard her tell Mom she wouldn't be caught dead knitting like some old Italian peasant.

How can you tell what's real? We all lied—Mom, Dad, Grams, An-ling, me. Whatever we were trying to save, it didn't work.

An-ling saw me that day in the park and winked at me. I pretended I didn't see her. I didn't want Mom to turn around. She was always asking me to stay with them, sit in on their talk. After An-ling left I would get, "Isn't she nice?" "Don't you like her?" "Please try to make her feel welcome. She has no family. Her home is far away."

"What about the Goo-Goo in San Francisco? She's got her."

Why did she wink at me in the park? I wanted to ask her, but I knew I never would. Was she making fun of me or making fun of Mom? And Mom reading poetry to her? I thought that was weird.

I think it was after seeing them in Riverside Park that I gave An-ling some space in my head. She was coming over for dinner two or three times a week, always on school nights. Dad said no to weekends. I thought it was because of the food. She and Mom always made Chinese food which Dad doesn't like. It wasn't as good as what you get at Ollie's over on 116th and Broadway, but it was better than takeout stews and meatloaf, which is what we eat most of the time.

During dinner, An-ling told stories about her life in a small village. Pretty grim ones. No running water, no heat. An outhouse. Her parents used to live in a big city—I forget the name. Her father was a well-known painter and her mother a doctor. During the Cultural Revolution, her mother was lucky to get work in a shoe factory, but her father was sent away to build dikes or something, and she said that when he came back after Mao died, his hands were bleeding stumps.

"Too much water." She made circles in the air with her arms.

"You mean a flood?" I said.

"Yes, a flood take his tools and the Red Guards make him dig with his hands."

Mom was drinking this stuff up, her face getting all soggy.

Dad put his fork down, chewed on his food real slow like he wasn't liking it a whole lot, swallowed, all the time keeping his eyes on a spot above An-ling's head. "The Cultural Revolution ended over thirty years ago," he said.

An-ling straightened up tall in her chair, her neck getting long, like she was trying to reach that spot Dad kept looking at. "This happen before me. My parents old when I come."

"I see."

When she left, he didn't wait long to say, "That girl made that whole story up."

Mom slapped the pot she was cleaning down on the counter. I was standing right next to her, drying, and got a big splash of dishwater all over me. "Hey, watch it!"

But she was only paying attention to Dad. "Why are you being so unpleasant? What has that sweet girl done to you?"

Dad walked out. That's when it hit me that Dad might be jealous.

An-ling had the strangest mouth. Most of us have a dip in the middle of the top lip. Hers was an arc, with no break. It was kinda cool. Her hair was yellow at first, the color of the legal pads Dad keeps on his desk. She hated her hair because it was thick and stiff. When she didn't have any money, she used to cut her own hair off to make paint brushes. That's what she said, but I think she made that one up too. It looked much prettier when Mom dyed it back to black.

Sometimes, when I was little, I'd dream that Mom wasn't my real mother, that Dad had an affair and I was the result.

That my real mother was killed by a drunk driver, or Dad wouldn't let her keep me. Sometimes she died giving birth to me. I hated those dreams, but they kept coming.

The time I got my first drum set—that was Mom's doing. I'd wanted it forever, but Dad kept bringing up the oboe, what a rich sound it had, how easy it was to carry around. I stopped asking after a while. Then on my tenth birthday, when I came home from school, sitting on top of my bed was a Tama Rockstar drum kit. "From Mom and Dad," the card said, but from the look on Dad's face, I knew it was all Mom's doing. Before An-ling came along, that was the best moment in my life.

I can help Mom. I want to help. I really do, but it's too hard.

Emma

It was late June. We had both taken the day off from work and ridden the ferry to visit Staten Island's botanical gardens.

"We are as close to ancient intellectual China as we can be in this country," An-ling said as I followed her to the Chinese Scholar's Garden. She was wearing a flowered cotton sundress and soft black Chinese slippers that reminded me of Mary Janes. Her dyed yellow hair was loose, thick against her cheeks.

"The scholar was on top of the heap in ancient China," she said. "A very big deal."

We walked up a few steps and stopped just inside the entrance in front of a large mahogany screen which hid the view beyond. "Steps stop the evil spirits." An-ling's face was serious, concentrated, filled with pride. Our roles reversed here, I was the foreigner, her student.

"Also the screen stops them. You will see. The garden path we follow waves like the tail of a tiger because evil spirits can only go in a straight line. The scholars had great good fortune, but if their performance was poor, ooh,"—she grimaced in mock pain—"very bad things happen to them."

We walked to the right, beyond the screen. To my surprise the garden was set up like a living space, a winding walled structure made up of enclosed rooms, pavilions and small courtyards surrounding a long pond.

"There were lotus blossoms once, but they died." Clusters of limestone and granite rocks, what the Chinese think of as the bones of the earth, rose out of the water like miniature mountains.

"Everything comes from China. Artisans and artists came over from Suzhou to build it." An-ling seemed to know this place by heart. She showed me the Tea House of Hearing Pines. "No glue, no nails. The wood is joined like this." She slipped her fingers into each other, held her crossed hands in front of her face. The beads of her bracelets caught the sun. "Like lovers."

The analogy embarrassed me. I have never thought of myself as a prude and yet I refused the picture of An-ling's legs wrapped around a man's hips.

"What does this mean?" I asked, pointing to the door handles, hoping there was no sexual connotation to their double curved shape.

"They are made to look like bats. They bring good luck. The word for bat sounds like *fu*, the word for good fortune."

An-ling took my hand and led me outside, through the Wandering in Bamboo Courtyard, half hidden behind walls with banana-leaf-shaped openings.

"A place to meditate," she said. A stand of bamboo blocked out the sun and bathed the courtyard in a yellow-green light. I felt I was underwater, swaying with the current, in a place without time.

"The garden has many spaces that catch you by surprise," An-ling said, without a trace of an accent. "Hidden views. Like in our hearts. Places where we go to be quiet, or places full of secrets which we don't show even to our best friends."

The green light flickered on her face with the movement of the bamboo leaves. Her face was expectant, waiting for some revelation. I walked out of the courtyard to follow a path that led me through a round opening in a wall. On the other side, beyond a shallow stepped bridge, a smaller pond rippled under a gentle waterfall.

"Listen to the water. Like the sound of the wind." An-ling offered me a smile and the quickness of it, its easy radiance, triggered suspicions. An-ling too had secrets.

A lawnmower started chewing loudly on the grass outside the garden.

"How long have you really lived in this country?"

An-ling shrugged and walked away. I followed her to the Moonviewing Pavilion, with its view of the surrounding greenery. She dropped down on a bench and leaned her head on the wooden railing. The mower was right below us, unbearably loud, pushed by a shirtless man, his tanned chest oiled with sweat under the relentless sun. An-ling followed the man's movement, a bird watching a cat.

"How long, An-ling?"

"Two sisters lived on the moon," she said. "They were too shy to accept so many lovers' eyes staring at them every night, so they asked their brother who lived on the sun to change places—"

"Tell me the truth. Please."

"He said many more looked at him"—the mower's infernal noise looped back, exploded below us—"but the sisters had a plan."

"An-ling, I want to know."

She waited until the mower moved away. "When I was fifteen I passed the teachers' exams and was sent to the college in Guangzhou to become a middle-school teacher. A Peace Corps teacher came to my school to teach us English. His name was Tom, like your husband. Tom had such a flat rear end we joked that he must have been a very bad boy for his father to hit him so hard. He was my first crush. Tom Owens." She paused while the mower churned past us again.

"After I graduated, I was supposed to go back to teach in my village and earn what for you would be thirty-five dollars a month. A classmate wanted me to go with her to work in a factory in Shenzhen, which was not too far. Near Hong Kong. The pay is very good, starting salary over eight-hundred a month, but the city is fenced in. No one can leave without permission, and you must work seven days a week and sleep only a few hours.

"I wrote to my aunt in San Francisco to bring me to the United States. I signed a promise on paper to work in her Chinese restaurant until I paid off my debt.

"Once, I called Boise, Idaho. Tom had left me his parents' address. His mother told me he was married and was a teacher in Seattle." An-ling brushed a lock of hair against her jawbone. "His wife was going to have a baby in two months."

She continued to brush her hair against her jaw. Her face betrayed no emotion.

"It must have been hard for you." I said. "All of it." I wondered if she had cut her wrists for love of Tom Owens.

"A year and half I worked for fourteen hours a day. For two hours a night and on my one day off I studied English, read the books out loud over and over to get rid of my accent. When I paid my debt to my aunt I came to New York." She attempted a breezy smile, as if to say her life had been easy, then bowed her head low, her hands joined on her lap. A penitent's pose.

"I saw the ad for your class in Chinatown. Free lessons. I was curious. Maybe I'd find another Tom to teach me more Shakespeare. When I saw your students, all new immigrants, I was ashamed for them, for what they didn't know, for how hungry they were for American words, American life.

"I put on a strong accent and pretended to be one of them. At the end, when everyone left, I could see in your eyes that you liked me, that you wanted to teach me. I could tell that. I was afraid you would be too angry if I told you the truth. That's why I didn't come back."

The mower was gone, replaced by the trill of a mockingbird and the swish of leaves caught in a breeze. "An-ling, dear, never worry about what I think. Relax, be young, carefree. Be happy."

Her head stayed down. "My lies make me ashamed. Please forgive me."

"I understand how difficult it's been for you. Now it's over; you're in the United States. I'll help you. I promise. You'll never have to lie to me again."

"Thank you, Lady Teacher—Emma." She looked up at me. The sadness flooding her face was so deep it made me feel powerless.

"Tell me what happened to the sisters on the moon," I said.

"The sisters and brother exchanged places and now we cannot look at the sun because the sisters will prick our eyes with their seventy-two embroidery needles." Her eyes scoured the clear sky. "We should stay and wait until the night to watch brother moon, but they won't let us."

I followed her to the walkway above the pond. She leaned over the railing and pointed to the koi, mere light streaks in the murky water. "In the old days, the ladies always sat by the water to mirror themselves."

I looked down. "What do you see?"

"A long line of women. My great-great-great-grandmother, great-great-grandmother, great-grandmother, grandmother, my mother, my aunts. The line grows, becomes thick. It rises and falls like the back of a dragon and like the dragon is too big for me to see all of him, the same with the women. I have to guess who they are from the parts I can see. I see knee bones worn down to wafers from washing the floors, backs bowed like the branches of the willow tree from planting rice, stumps of flesh that were feet, crushed to be beautiful in the eyes of their husbands. I

see my mother being dragged across the floor of her factory like a mop because she has dared to say that Mao does
not love his people.

"What do you see, Lady Teacher?"

"A beautiful young girl in America with a good life in
front of her." Our faces reflected in the water were like two
moons resting side by side at the bottom of the pond. Our
features blurred in the dirty water, and for a sweet moment
I pretended that we shared the same features, that we could
recognize ourselves in each other's faces, that I had given
birth to her.

SIX

Emma

THE FIRST SATURDAY of the trial, the windows of the apartment were open to the sunny day and a breeze climbed up from the river. Tom was making pancakes. I squeezed orange juice and ground the coffee while Josh set the kitchen table. If we had been caught on camera, we would have come across as an average family getting on with our safe, boring lives. The racing beat of fear doesn't show up on film.

"Yummy pancakes." I dug in to please Tom, to stay in the scene.

Josh stared at his fork, the pancakes on the plate in front of him untouched.

"I love you, Josh," I said. Tom lowered *The Economist* to smile his approval. Since I had come back from living with An-ling I kept breaking new ground with my effusiveness. "I love you very much. Both of you."

"How about eggs?" I added, to break the embarrassment we were all feeling. "French toast?"

"Naw, this is good." Josh stooped over his plate, tried two forkfuls, stopped, looked to see how much his father and I had eaten, how much longer he had to sit with us.

I waved my hand toward the door. "Go if you want to." Josh hesitated, waiting for his father's reaction.

Tom stood up, his food also unfinished. "I've got work to do. It's about time I reorganized the library." He ruffled my hair as he went by, patted Josh's shoulder, leaving his mark. Josh waited for Tom's footsteps to recede before getting up. He had grown taller in the past few months and as I sat below him, I felt small, defenseless and, for a lovely, reassuring instant, I felt that my son was the one trying to protect me.

"Come to the basement with me, Mom. I want to show you something." Suddenly he looked nervous, which frightened me.

"What is it, Josh?" He was already halfway across the room. "What do you want to show me?"

"I'm going to play some music for Mom," he shouted to Tom as he passed the study.

Tom was blowing dust from two tomes in his hands, face flushed from the effort. "Don't be too long. I could use some help from both of you."

"Use the vacuum cleaner, Tom," I said, hurrying after a loping Josh.

In the basement, he waited for me to step inside the room, then locked the door behind me. I steeled myself for what might come. He stood rigid in front of me. "What is it, Josh?"

"An-ling, she had a laptop."

"Yes, I know. An old beat-up one she bought from a classmate at the Art Students League. Why?" I knew the reason for his statement, but wanted him to tell me, to cross the divide between us.

"Did the police take it?"

"It's in the East River."

Josh's body sagged in what I could only suppose was relief.

"Why is the laptop important, Josh?"

He reached into a carrying case for one of his drums and handed me a sealed manila envelope.

"What's this?"

His eyes skirted away from me. "I'm sorry, Mom."

My breath and my heartbeat slowed, as if my body needed to conserve energy for what was to come. Faced with what could be another horrible surprise, another betrayal, I didn't want to know anything. And yet I had to ask, "What's in the envelope, Josh?"

"An-ling, she sent you e-mails."

I pushed the envelope back against his chest. "Not funny, Josh."

"She did! Look for yourself. She sent you e-mails with a company called BetterLateThanNever. They store your e-mails in their server and send them when you want."

I opened the envelope. Inside were eight, maybe ten e-mails from Chinesecanary@BetterLateThanNever.com. I let out a loud breath. Whatever blow I had expected, it wasn't this. I pushed aside Josh's music sheets and perched on a corner of the trunk next to his drum kit. What shattering words had she written? How much more guilt could I carry?

"If the e-mails were sent to me, how did you get hold of these? How did you know about them in the first place?"

He cringed.

"You were curious," I said. "You figured out my password and went on a scouting mission. What were you hoping to find, Josh? Tell me. I'm not angry. Really I'm not."

He met my gaze, his expression again unreadable.

"You don't get me, do you, Mom?"

"I try. I'm sorry." Now his anger was clearly etched on his face, and it brought out my own, if only because he was right. "Correct me. Tell me how you got these e-mails."

"You and Dad both, what the fuck was the idea of keeping the fact that I had a sister secret?" By then her death had been splattered all over the papers. "What the fuck, huh?"

"Please don't use that kind of lan—"

"Why didn't you tell me? It's like—"

"You're right, Josh. It was a terrible mistake. Your Dad and I thought—"

"It's like you and Dad never wanted me to get close." His face was red, the muscles of his neck taut. "Like what happens to you has nothing to do with me. You know what it feels like, this whole thing—Amy, An-ling, you on trial? It feels like one of those suicide bombers just exploded in my face and I just want to—" He turned his back to me, head bent.

I stepped forward and tried to hold him, but he slid away. "We didn't tell you about Amy because her death was too painful. We wanted to start from scratch with you. If we had told you, what would you have thought of us? How could you have loved us?"

Josh sat behind his drums, picked up his sticks.

"Please forgive us, honey. We thought silence was the best way."

He kept his head down. "An-ling called me the day she died. My cell was off. She left a message. That's how I found out about the e-mails."

Grief, cold and clammy, gripped my body. "What else did she say?"

"She left the e-mail company's number and asked me to wait six months before calling them. She said she would be in China by then and you'd be just about forgetting her after six months. That's all."

"What time did she call?"

"I don't know. That day." His eyes stayed on the drums.

"Did you read them?"

He shook his head, releasing a curl of hair from his pony-tail. He has to have read An-ling's e-mails, I told myself. Whatever she may have written, it couldn't matter anymore. I reached over and he let me stroke his neck.

"I waited until now to call the company—"

"Until the trial started," I finished for him. In case the e-mails held incriminating evidence. The D.A.'s office was now confident in its case against me. It no longer needed to go on fishing expeditions.

"I erased them from your hard drive," Josh said. "Just in case. That's why I broke in and printed them out. Max has special software I borrowed. What she wrote is gone, wiped out. You've got the only copy."

"You did nothing to harm her. You hear me, Josh? Nothing. I'm to blame. Only me." I kissed his hair, his shoulder. I smelled shampoo, fabric softener, maple syrup, the everyday smells of our lives as a family. I must memorize them, lock them inside my mind, I thought. In case . . .

"She didn't want you to forget her," he said. "Maybe the e-mails will make you feel better?"

Would Josh ever feel better? His whole life was now a question mark. Was I the only one to blame for that? I would have asked God, but I was no longer sure He was there to listen.

"Of course they will. Thank you, Josh, and thank you for not letting the police get hold of them."

He tried to smile. "That way no one knows. I didn't tell Dad. You and me share secrets now, huh?" He jiggled his leg up and down; his body shook with the force of it. "I didn't read them, Mom, I swear. I started to, but I couldn't. It hurt too much."

I hugged him. "I threw the St. Christopher medal in the river too."

Big, wet slurps of sound broke up Josh's shaking. "I'm so sorry, Mom," Josh cried and I drowned.

That same night, with Tom and Josh asleep, I sat on the rim of the bathtub, behind a locked door and read An-ling's first e-mail.

Subj: Fairytales and fantasies
Date: 04-06-05 13:32:46 EST
From: Chinesecanary@BetterLateThanNever.com
To: EPerotti@aol.com

A verse from the long-ago poet Shitao: "Oars striking the water stir the white clouds, setting bits of them afloat."

I will stir and set the white clouds, my lies, floating.

I've lied about a lot of things, but never about this. I love you like I love my mother. If I were in China I would go to the Yellow River valley and climb the 7,000 steps of the Broad Way to Heaven on my knees and ask the sacred Mount Tai the favor of your love back. That's what I'd do. Instead I write e-mails that you'll get only after I go away. You'll read them and laugh or cry. I don't know. What I'm doing is stupid, I guess. I don't know.

I'd like to tell you the truth. My truth, if I haven't lost it.

I think sometimes people lie for hope.

A-l

Josh

I read what An-ling wrote. I was sure she was going to talk about me, maybe lie about that too, make things look a lot worse than they were. Some of it was pretty embarrassing, not stuff you want your mother to read. Halfway through I made up my mind I was going to delete the e-mails. There was no way Mom would know they existed. I went on reading.

You think you know someone. You count on that person being the way you've made them out to be. You count on it. That's how you get by. Mom, Dad, Grams, my friend Max, An-ling, they're with me all the time, sort of like doorways that take you somewhere, lead you forward, but you always know you can stop in one, look around, take five if you need to.

Mom. She wasn't always there for me. I'd catch her with this look on her face—like she was bored with me. When I was little I kept telling myself she was tired and I'd stop myself from crying. It made me mad sometimes. It was Dad who tucked me in at night, read to me while she stood by the door. I used to think she couldn't wait to get away from me. "Mom and I love you very much," Dad always said before turning out the light. I was never sure about the Mom part. I didn't know I had a dead sister then, that Mom killed her.

It's always been Dad. He's tried real hard to make everything okay.

I was going to delete the e-mails, but then I remembered Grams telling me that Dad burned all of my sister's clothes, toys, all the pictures, so there was nothing left to help Mom remember. It didn't feel right to do that to her all over again. And maybe, if she read those e-mails, Mom would see that An-ling wasn't a perfect person, that she lied a lot, and then she wouldn't miss her so much. That's what I was thinking while I was reading them. I was also thinking that maybe An-ling wanted me to make the call because she really was planning to be in China, but the last thing she said in the message was, "Drummer boy, I'm scared." Maybe she knew she might die.

Mom's lawyer, Mr. Fishkin, thinks he's got a pretty tight defense. The D.A.'s office only has circumstantial evidence, he says. They can't prove motive. Dad seems pretty sure Mom's going to get off, too. I told BetterLateThanNever to send An-ling's e-mails five months ago, right after Mom was indicted and the police got out of our hair. It took me that long to know what to do. Now she has them. Except the last one. That one I burned.

Subj: Fairytales and fantasies
Date: 04-07-05 10:05:00 EST
From: Chinesecanary@BetterLateThanNever.com
To: EPerotti@aol.com

I was happy you came looking for me at Feldy's office. I started going to your apartment building after the night you let me ride in the taxi with you. I waited for you to come home. I hid behind one of the big trees across the street, at the entrance to the park.

One time I found courage and planted myself under the streetlamp, hoping you'd see me. A boy swerved to a stop in front of you as you came around the corner. A head taller than you on his roller blades, skinny beneath his floppy T-shirt. You talked to each other for a minute, no more. No kiss, no touching, but I guessed he was your son, Josh. You love him very much, I thought. I waited on the sidewalk, wanted to wave, call out, but he was there. I wanted you to invite me into your happy home. I knew it was happy because of the Hudson River—a flowing stream in front of a home brings riches and success.

I am a foolish girl born in a house with stagnant water.

I didn't know you were looking for me. No one has come looking for me with good in their heart. Before you, no one.

A-l

Emma

With An-ling's words, more memories:

Over our cereal bowls, Tom and I were fighting. I wanted An-ling to come with us on vacation in August. Two weeks in Alaska—a landscape we'd never seen, that An-ling had never imagined. I wanted all of us to discover it together. She filled me with Chinese legends, Chinese ways. What I could offer her was a different corner of my country, the breadth and variety of its beauty. But Tom wouldn't have her; An-ling was an intrusion. I had explained, at night, the two of us lying on separate edges of the bed, speaking quietly so Josh wouldn't hear, how An-ling's presence delighted me, how helping her helped me feel good again. My words meant nothing to Tom.

I dropped my spoon in the ceramic bowl and relished the jarring clang, my small act of rebellion. "Why not? I'll have some company while you and Josh go off on one of your grueling hikes. I'll pay her expenses out of my salary if that's what's worrying you."

"There's no division of income in our family. What I earn is yours and vice versa. It's not a question of money."

"What then? You pride yourself on your generosity, in giving to charities. Why can't you be generous to An-ling? Why do you dislike her so much?"

I got no answer. Tom doesn't like us to argue in front of Josh. He's right, but in the face of his stubbornness I couldn't let go of my own.

"She hasn't asked anything of us. She doesn't impose herself. It's been all my doing."

"That's exactly the point. You're obsessing over a girl who has nothing to do with us."

" 'Us' who? Us family? Us Americans?" Tom had lost his father in the Korean War when he was five years old and for all I knew he hated all Asians. He often accused me of keeping my true self under lock and key, but he too hid pockets of emotion in places I couldn't reach.

" 'I' want An-ling to go on vacation with an American family, and my wish should at least be taken into consideration, instead of being dismissed the minute it comes out of my mouth. I am part of that 'us' you like to vaunt."

" 'Us' is family, Emma. Josh, you and me. If you need a name for what I feel, let's say it's disappointment." With that statement he made his exit, leaving me with his empty cereal bowl.

Disappointment. It's an anger-deflating word. It stole my confidence. I had no answer to it.

Josh stayed hunched over his plate of microwaved waffles, his head cocked toward the open kitchen door. When the sleigh bells at the front door jangled twice, the signal that Tom had left, Josh said, "Dad's been working real hard." His sweetness moved me.

"Do you mind if An-ling comes with us to Alaska?" I asked. "You can tell me the truth." Josh loves his steadfast father deeply, is sternly loyal to him, will never contradict him. And yet I hoped.

Josh shuffled out of his chair, and lowered his plate in the sink. "I don't care. I'm going to be late." He grabbed a banana from the hanging basket.

We both knew he had plenty of time. "Only empty plates in the sink, please, Josh." I picked up his plate, scraped the nibbled remains of the waffles into the garbage can. "You like An-ling, don't you?"

"Yeah, sure. I don't care. You and Dad fight it out. What I think isn't going to change your mind."

"That's not true!" Part of me was shocked by the accusation; most of me felt instantly guilty. I accused back. "I don't know what you think. I ask, but you never tell me. You always defer to your father. What he says goes. Don't let him do that to you, Josh. Stand up for whatever it is you want."

I wasn't being fair; my anger at Tom was spilling over onto Josh, but I couldn't stop myself. The truth is they deferred to each other on most things. Sometimes I felt as though the Berlin Wall were still standing, right in our apartment. Josh and Tom on one side and me on the other. They were the couple, they completed each other's sentences. They gave me gifts in tandem, turning me into the child. What I was, to Tom and maybe to Josh, was the renegade element, not to be counted on. I was the one who had set it up this way; I was the one who regretted it.

"What do you want, Josh?"

THE PRICE OF SILENCE

"Convince Dad to get me a home gym. I can put it down in the basement room." His look was pleading. The home gym was going to make all the difference in his life. He'd reached the age where his body mattered. Before long he'd be into necking with some girl on the sofa while we were at the movies.

"Dad thinks it's too expensive. Can't you work out at school?"

"Please, Mom. It's only eight hundred dollars."

More or less the cost of taking An-ling with us to Alaska. Was that what he was thinking?

"You and Dad can give it to me for my birthday."

Was I being offered a trade-off? A home gym for An-ling coming to Alaska? "I'm not very good at changing Dad's mind," I said.

"Yes, you are. I got a drum kit instead of an oboe."

I was uncomfortable with this request.

"You can give it to me for my birthday *and* Christmas."

Josh and Tom were my family. Their wishes should have come before An-ling. But I see now that what Tom called my "obsession" had only partly to do with An-ling. Yes, I wanted to give that lost, grieving, fragile child the life my Amy should have had. A crazy part of me thought that by helping An-ling I was making it up to my real daughter. That, wherever she was, Amy would understand and maybe even forgive me.

But what Tom and I did not fully realize was that at that point I had already been sitting in the defendant's seat for more years than I could take.

Subj: Fairytales and fantasies
Date: 04-08-05 17:34:06 EST
From: Chinesecanary@BetterLateThanNever.com
To: EPerotti@aol.com

I never expected you to stay with me. So much kindness is not for girls like me. What I want to say, Lady Teacher, is that for a little while you made me feel that my feet made firm contact with the ground. My arms were strong in their movement. The air made way for me when I walked and its soft whisper gathered in the marrow of my bones. I will always be grateful.

I am a black and white koi in the stream.
Sunlight flashes on my scales.
The world sees me dance with joy.

A-I

In class I asked my students to read out loud from the previous day's *Daily News*. After my argument with Tom, I was in no mood to teach grammar rules or listen to the personal anecdotes I had asked them to write out the night before. At the end of class, Esmeralda, my best reader, protested that I had let Vicki read four paragraphs to her two. "Her speaking is terrible. You don't listen, Miss Emma." She too was disappointed in me. On an impulse I gave her the Waterman pen she always borrowed to write her class essays. Only after she had left and the room filled with my advanced students did I remember the pen was an old birthday gift from Tom.

In my next class I asked my students to use their fifty minutes to write an essay on the person who had had or still had the most meaning in their lives. When class was over—it was noon on a Thursday, the one day I taught only in the morning—I walked toward my cubicle and found An-ling at the end of the corridor, gathering papers from the copy machine. I hadn't seen her since our visit to the Chinese Scholar's Garden a week earlier.

The unexpectedness of her visit was a splash of cool air on a stifling day and I hung back to savor the surprise. She wore a shiny flowered skirt and a black halter top that left her midriff and back bare, and I was taken aback by how poised she seemed, how self-assured. Away from her, my thoughts turned An-ling into a shy, fragile girl. A girl who wore bracelets to hide the scars on her wrists. A girl gaping with need.

"You look like you're going off on a vacation," I said, approaching her. "Did you take a day off?"

An-ling pecked my cheeks and handed me a tube of candy from the pocket of her skirt. "To make the day sweet," she said.

I popped a cherry Life Saver into my mouth and asked, "To what do I owe this wonderful visit?"

"Good friends do not keep secrets from each other. You wanted to see where I live. I will show you."

I felt flattered, elated. I dropped my students' essays in my cubicle and grabbed my handbag and jacket. "Let's get out of here."

We rode two subway trains. On the way she fished into her tote bag and showed me sheet after sheet of paper on which she had copied her face. An expanse of white for her cheek, tiny pores showing, her profile silhouetted against the rigid glass. A furrowed streak of white for her forehead in a frontal shot, her nose a light bulbous splotch, her eyes dark recesses, her hair a zig-zag of floating lines. After seeing only a few, I handed them back, repelled. They seemed the pictures of a corpse.

"I hope you kept your eyes closed. The light can hurt you."

She laughed, showing off her perfect teeth. "You are so American thinking, so sweet with your worry voice."

"Are the copies for new art work?" She must have used up half a ream.

"I want to fix my face, to pin it down like a butterfly, to see the inside. Self-portraits are so hard. I must learn, take more classes. My face betrays me. It says I am Chinese, but if I go back to China they will not accept me. I am marked by the white ghost, the Westerner. There is something different about a Chinese raised here. Amy Tan says so. In China they know."

"But you weren't raised here."

Her face shuttered down. She didn't like being corrected. She would have been a difficult student, I had come to realize. "I'm no longer Chinese; I'm not American. I am *wy gwo ren*, an outside country person. In this new state, I am like bamboo in a strong wind. I have no signs of my past, of my ancestry, to mark the road for me. I'm like the lion cubs that are thrown down the valley. Only the strong ones make it back up the mountain and deserve to be king of the beasts."

I looked around at the other passengers in our subway car. Her disorientation, her sense of loss, were shared by a lot of them, I wanted to tell her—but I remembered my own stubbornness in my suffering, my need to feel that what I was going through was unique in this world, how friends' attempts to point out other people's similar suffering had seemed to diminish my own and brought no comfort at all.

It was freezing in the subway car. An-ling's arms were covered in goosebumps. I wrapped my jacket around her. "You're Chinese-American the way I'm Italian-American," I said. "To have two cultures is something to be proud of."

"Hyphens divide, hyphens unite. I don't care. The most important thing is,"—she raised an arm, fingers spread high, a player shooting for the basket—"the important thing is I am making it up the mountain!"

Her optimism delighted me. I had no doubts that she would reach her goals.

Her apartment was on a Queens street filled with two-story warehouses. No grocery store, no laundry, nothing that would indicate it was a residential neighborhood. Mid-block, An-ling unlocked a large metal door which opened onto a loading dock. Inside, we made our way through a maze of sealed cartons to a metal staircase.

"What's inside these?" I asked.

"My staying here is not legal. I ask no questions." We walked up to the second floor. At the end of a narrow hallway she unlocked a padlock. I followed her into a small windowless kitchen. A deep double-sink—the kind found in the laundry rooms of century-old houses—took up half of one wall. Next to it, a table held a hot plate. An outsized refrigerator filled most of the rest of the room.

"A photographer used to work here," she said.

The kitchen opened into a tight rectangle at the end of which a grimy window smacked against the brick wall of the next building. On the concrete floor under the window there was a futon and a stool with a lamp on it. There was no other furniture in the room. The walls were covered with paintings whose subject matter I couldn't make out. At one o'clock on a summer afternoon the room was too dark, with no ceiling light. In one wall, a door stood open, revealing a closet-sized room that contained a toilet and nothing else. The air in the apartment was stale, filled with the smell of paint. My heart shriveled to see how An-ling lived.

"Turn on the lamp. I want to see your paintings." I used my cheerful teacher's voice, which didn't fool her.

"It's a matter of perspective," An-ling said. "The kitchen has running water. I have a toilet I can flush. New York is outside my window, the ocean not very far away." She removed the lamp and offered me the stool to sit on. Through the window I glimpsed an inch-wide sliver of sunlit street.

An-ling sat cross-legged on the futon. "On my tenth birthday my mother took me to the South China Sea. It was not far, two hours on the bus. When we got to the beach, my mother held my head and made me look out as far as I could see.

" 'A frog in a well cannot imagine the size of the ocean,' she said. 'The ocean is a gift. See. Listen. Smell. Tie the ocean with a ribbon and hide it in your head. When you are in the dark, you will open your gift and the ocean will keep you company.'

"She knew about the dark, sewing soles on shoes for eighteen hours a day, six days a week. She knew also I would end up in this room.

"It's small and dark like the bottom of a well, but the rain doesn't come in and the floor is large enough for my futon. The wall is my easel and in my head I have the ocean wrapped in a ribbon."

It's too dark, I wanted to tell her. You can't paint here.

I left the stool, snapped on the lamp and peered at the large canvases within the reach of its light. The strokes were sure, the oil paint thick, with none of the delicacy and meticulousness I'd seen in old Asian paintings. She painted everyday objects, both Chinese and Western, piled high like mountains. A turquoise fan with dancing girls on it thrown on top of a pile of envelopes addressed in script next to a man's belt coiled in a nest of silk scarves below a wide-necked blue vase filled with brightly colored women's high-heeled shoes. Another painting was dedicated to the kitchen: pots, pans, a wok, chopsticks, a cleaver, Brillo pads, cellophane-wrapped Chinese noodles spilling out of a basket. I let out a laugh of surprise when I recognized the green-lidded jar I use to store my tea. Each painting depicted a human body part: a hand holding the fan, a nose peeking out of a glass, an elbow resting in the middle of the man's belt.

"These paintings are wonderful, full of humor," I said.

Her face opened up with pleasure. "Thank you. Until the last century, oil painting was not accepted in China, but it's more powerful than watercolor or ink, and it doesn't wash away."

"You have so much talent, An-ling. You should make the rounds of galleries."

She stood up. "Stay here, I will make tea."

I watched her silently glide across the floor in her bare feet. I wanted more than anything else to give An-ling shelter, but she was like a deer, full of grace, poised to flee at the least movement of possession.

She rested against the door jamb as we waited for the water to boil. "There's a legend that says that Chinese painting was invented by a woman. One day, Fu Li saw that her favorite songbird had flown away from its cage. She waited every day for it to come back, sent her servants out to look for it in the vast gardens of the palace.

"Shun, her brother, the great ruler, offered Fu Li the best songbirds in the province, but she wanted her favorite songbird back, no other. Shun asked his scribes to write amusing stories to cheer his sister up." Her voice was sure, level. It was a story she knew well.

"When the first scroll arrived, its ink was still wet. The scribe had been in a great hurry to get it ready before nightfall. Instead of reading it, Fu Li cried and cried and her tears smeared the ink." The tea kettle whistled. An-ling disappeared, raising her voice.

"In the smear Fu Li saw the wing of a bird and with a wet finger she pushed the ink this way and that way and soon enough she had painted the image of her beloved songbird. To the end of her days she kept her ink bird near her, swearing she could hear it sing."

An-ling crossed the floor with two cups of dense black tea.

"I like that story. It's optimistic." I took a sip. The tea was too strong, bitter. "Bringing back a loved one with tears and a little ink."

Carefully balancing her cup, An-ling lowered herself onto the futon. "My grandmother told me that story after she sold my father's paintings. The story was meant to honor women painters, but my grandmother liked it because it showed how foolish girls can be with their imagination, with their need to see something for what it isn't. She had no use for painting. 'You cannot eat it,' she liked to say. 'It will not keep you warm in the winter.'

"I told her she was the foolish one. My father's paintings fed her." An-ling drew her knees to her chest. "I have something else to show you."

She opened a sketchbook that had been under her futon and dropped a black-and-white photograph in my lap. It fit easily in the palm of my hand. A little girl, standing next to a stone lion three times her size, peered at the camera. She wore a fancy light-colored jacket and pants ringed with dark bands. Her hair was in a long ribboned braid on one side of her head.

"That is me at the Moon Festival. It's our Thanksgiving."

The picture was yellowed, faded, grainy, as if taken with a dirty camera lens. "How old are you here?"

"Five. My mother took the photo. I ate so many cakes that night I threw up on my outfit and Mama was very angry with me, but she didn't hit me. She was too educated." I heard immense pride in her voice.

"You must miss her terribly."

"It's the only photo I have of me in China." She showed me another photo. "This is my mother."

The eight-by-ten portrait of a young woman with a square jaw and a tight mouth reminded me of the unsmiling photos of subway supervisors posted near the token booths. "She doesn't look like you."

"That is a photo from the factory where she made shoes for Chairman Mao. She was pretty when she was happy."

"I'm sorry," I said, the most useless words in the English language, but that is what I genuinely felt: sorrow for her, for her losses. "Thank you for showing me these photos." I glanced at her wrists, sheathed as always in the beaded bracelets. "An-ling, if there is anything more you want to tell me, I'm here to listen."

She slipped the photos back into the sketchbook and unhooked a bracelet. "For you." She held it close to my face. I saw now that it was new, covered with whirls of tiny pink and purple glass beads, not a family heirloom at all.

"I can't accept it."

"You're always staring at my bracelets. I think you want them. Come on, it's Canal Street cheap. We'll share. One for me one for you." There was something provocative in the way she spoke. I wondered if she knew I'd seen what the bracelet hid.

"Thank you, An-ling, but no. Your bracelets are very pretty and they look wonderful on you." Where did the desperation come from, I wanted to ask? But there are invisible boundaries in all friendships that shouldn't be crossed. My desperation, hers. Off limits.

An-ling hooked the bracelet, obviously glad the moment was over, the matter dropped. "I quit Feldy. It's very stupid work pulling faces."

I laughed with relief at this good news, at the hurdle we'd just crossed. "That's great. You should be painting every day, taking more classes. Do you want a part-time job? Maybe I can help you find one."

"You are always too good to me. I have money saved. When I need more I'll model for the art schools, maybe get a permit to sell paintings in front of the museums."

"If I can help, please—"

An-ling pressed a strand of her yellow hair against my mouth.

"Be my friend. That is all I need."

On the way home, I stopped at Paragon and bought Josh his home gym.

SEVEN

Subj: Fairytales and fantasies
Date: 04-08-05 17:02:00 EST
From: Chinesecanary@BetterLateThanNever.com
To: EPerotti@aol.com

In China a man is born, grows up and dies in the same house. He never has to leave his home or his parents. A woman leaves family and home. When her husband-to-be comes to her family house to take her to the marriage ceremony, her father throws a bucket of water on the path her feet have just left. The hard earth receives the water with a loud slap, separates it, runs it off into streams that stretch thin until they disappear. You cannot take back thrown-away water. It's gone forever. So it is with a daughter.

You were my new home. That was my hope.

It was Josh who told me about Amy, what he knew from his grandmother. I came early for dinner. You weren't home from school yet. Tom I guess was at work. Josh took me down to the basement to show me his drums. I told him that during the mid-autumn festival the drums get beaten to hurry up the blooming of the flowers. We started playing a game from the festival. The drummer beats the drum. When he stops, who holds the wine cup must drink. Josh opened the bottle of Italian wine meant for you with his Swiss Army knife and we took turns drinking, beating the drum. He told me about his sister. I thought he was going to cry and I hugged him. He smelled more of chewing gum than wine.

This is true. All of what I'm writing to you is true. It's too late for lies.

A-l

Tom

Eight months after Amy's death, Emma announced she was pregnant. Before I could express my happiness at the wonderful news, she cut me off cold. "I'm having an abortion."

"I'll never agree to it."

"I don't need your permission."

"It's my child, too."

"Then you carry it. Scream your head off when it splits you in two. Then nurse your baby, love her so much it takes your breath away and then when she dies, what will you do then, Tom? Go for one more? Why not, have another one like you have another Scotch!"

"You can't do this to us, Emma."

"I'll go crazy if I don't. The date is set. I will not have another child. Ever."

I accused her of wanting to be miserable, of wearing suffering like a halo, of feeling virtuous because of it. "All you need is a palm frond in your hand and you'd be the perfect martyr!"

I brought Father Caputi home to ram some piety into her.

"Amy's death was our personal original sin," she told him, "something we have to expiate for the rest of our lives. There's no place for a new birth or even our rebirth." Nothing he could say would change her mind.

I threatened divorce, believing my role as husband, partner, still had leveraging power. I stuffed all of Amy's belongings into black garbage bags and drove them to the town dump. I scraped off the striped wallpaper in her room, the bunny rabbit border. Emma looked down at the green strips covering the carpet and said she felt flayed.

"God damn it, Emma, I want that baby. We're being given another chance!"

Ten days later I came home from teaching and she had changed her mind. I didn't risk asking why.

This time there was no miscarriage, no six weeks in bed. The baby was born after less than an hour of labor. Before Emma came home from the hospital I removed all of the pictures of Amy from the house and told her I had burned them. I was trying to help Emma direct her love to the future, to our son. I chose the name Joshua; Emma agreed. I even bought him a trumpet, foolishly thinking his birth would crumble Emma's wall of grief.

One truth that guides me is that I love my son above anyone or anything else. I will do whatever is necessary to keep him safe, to make sure I am there when he needs me.

Sergeant Daniel is on the stand. He is a thirty-three-year veteran of the police force, a tall, large African American with a soft face and drooping eyelids that give him a tired, worn look. He sets his eyes on Ms. Perotti's son, Josh, sitting on a spectator bench. There is compassion on his face.

"You are the detective in charge of this case?"

"I am."

"When did you first interview the defendant?"

"On April twenty-first of last year."

"Can you briefly tell the jury what transpired during that first interview."

"I showed Ms. Perotti the crime scene photos showing the dead body and then asked her about her relationship to—"

Josh

I wish he'd stop gawking at me. Just because we talked a little about music, no way are we pals.

Mom had been back home about ten days when the doorbell rang. I expected it to be Mrs. Ricklin from down the hall; I walk her dog two times a day. Instead a big man in a suit and a bow tie filled the whole doorway. Al Roker, that's who this guy looked like. Al Roker when he was fat. A nice-guy face. An-ling had been dead about a week is my guess.

"Is your mother or father home?"

"No." I was wondering why Julio, the doorman, hadn't buzzed to say this guy was coming up.

"When are they coming back?"

Down the hall, Mrs. Ricklin was calling me. "Joshy, Joshy, Scottie needs to go out. It's late, Joshy." Mrs. Ricklin is eighty-two years old and I guess she can call me anything she likes.

"I'll be right there!"

In my head I thanked her for being deaf so that I had to shout and my voice didn't give away how scared I was. Four guys were waiting down the hall by Mrs. Ricklin's apartment and two of them carried satchels with NYPD written on them. One beanpole guy I recognized from the police station in Brooklyn. Last week he'd taken my fingerprints along with Dad's. "Just routine," he'd said and I'd gotten through it without breaking into a sweat by pretending I was in a TV show—*CSI, Law and Order, NYPD Blue*, take your pick, anything that wasn't real. Now the guy was back and I was glad Mrs. Ricklin wasn't wearing her glasses. The men and the NYPD logos on the satchels could only be a blur to her.

"Who's there, Joshy?"

I meant to answer her right away, but it was like I was standing in front of a huge crowd expecting me to hit the drums, but I couldn't remember any music. My stomach was flip-flopping all over the place and I was sure it was showing on my face and this man—the guy on the witness stand now—would think I had something to tell him. By then Scottie was barking.

"It's all right, Mrs. Ricklin. They're friends of Dad's." I reached for my jacket hanging by the door and stuck my arms in it. "I've got to walk her dog or he's going to shit all over her rug."

I had to squeeze out the door because the man didn't budge. I locked the door behind me, called out, "Come on, boy." Scottie raced to me down the hall.

The man intercepted, started playing with him, tugging at the leash in Scottie's mouth, spinning the dog around, lifting him off the ground. Scottie growled with pleasure and I felt totally betrayed.

On one of the spins I grabbed the dog. "He's really got to go, sir." The man let go of the leash. I clipped it to Scottie's collar and shouted to Mrs. Ricklin that I was going to take her dog on a nice long run along the river. "It may take an hour, so don't worry."

The policemen followed me down the stairs. All five of them. The big man introduced himself as Sergeant Daniel, sticking his badge under my nose while I skipped down the stairs two at time.

"My parents aren't coming home until late," I lied. "They're going to a dinner and a movie. I don't know where." I could tell he was having trouble with the stairs and I didn't slow down. "They gave me money for takeout." I showed him a twenty dollar bill from my pocket, just in case he thought they were terrible parents or something.

In the lobby he told his guys to wait in their cars; he was going with me. "Scottie needs to run," I reminded him, but that didn't phase him. The beanpole guy wanted to come with us, but Sergeant Daniel said no, he was just going for a walk, nothing more. If he thought he was going to catch me off guard—just-the-two-of-us-and-the-dog-taking-a-

THE PRICE OF SILENCE

nice-stroll-in-the-park kind of thing—he didn't know anything about teenagers. We're a lot smarter than we make out
to be.

We crossed the street into Riverside Park. Scottie left his
mark on every tree on our way down to the Hudson.
Sergeant Daniel walked with a rock-in-the-shoe lean to his
left. When we passed our first bench I asked him if he wanted to sit down and untie his shoe. I don't know why I did
that. If his foot was hurting him, he didn't need me to tell him
what to do. Maybe I was trying to show him what a nice guy
I was. He laughed at my question and kept on going.

"You've got a search warrant with you, right?" I said.
"What are you looking for? An-ling hasn't been in our
apartment in months and months." Scottie started pulling at
his leash and barking wildly. I jerked him back. "Shut up!"
He can't stand squirrels.

"Why don't you just ask Dad? He'll let you in. We've got
nothing to hide." He could even look down in my room in
the basement. There was nothing there yet that had anything to do with An-ling.

"Your father has a very poor view of the police."

Who wouldn't? They were harassing Mom and then two
detectives showed up at Dad's office without calling first.
One of his students came in the waiting room and overheard An-ling's name and some of the questions and spread
the news that the police were questioning Professor
Howells in the Asian artist murder case. As a result, three students dropped out of his class; the Dean called him into his
office to discuss damage control and now Dad wanted to
sue the police.

I'd been asked questions too, after the fingerprinting.

Q: How well did you know An-ling?

A: Not much. I only saw her when she'd come over to see my mother.

Q: Never alone?

A: Once she came down to the basement to see my drum set.

Q: Did you ever go to the studio?

A: No.

Q: Never?

A: No.

Q: Do you have any idea who had a grudge against An-ling? Did she ever mention how she came to the States? Do you know if she had another name?

No. No. No.

My arm jerked. Scottie was choking on his leash and a squirrel leaped up the tree to safety. "You're not even close to finding her killer, are you? That's why you're coming to our apartment with a search warrant. You're desperate."

Sergeant Daniel didn't even blink. "You should think of becoming a detective when you grow up, but you're going to be a percussionist, I hear. At least that's what your mother thinks. Is that how you see it?"

Mom discussing me with a detective? What else did she tell him? "I'm not good enough. I don't know."

"Billy Higgins. He made a name for himself playing on Ornette Coleman's early recordings. Smiling Billy. You ever heard him?"

I shook my head.

"Get one of his CDs and listen good. You'll learn a lot. He wasn't one of those show-off players who need people to break out clapping and hooting in the middle of the piece to tell them how great they are. I hope you don't need that when you play, because in the end it doesn't serve the music and the music is what playing is all about."

"Making the music shine," I said. Playing is also about stepping out of the world and finding you've become someone else, like a swimmer when he dives into a pool and starts moving his body through the water and suddenly he's become this incredibly beautiful fish without any weight to him. "Making the music shine."

We were walking along the river by now and Sergeant Daniel told me how he loved the smell of sun mixed with water when the weather got warm, how the smell reminded him of eating his mother's fish stew when he was a boy younger than me. Then he said how sad it must have been for me when Mom left to live with An-ling. How it must have made me angry too. A girl she'd known for just a short time becoming more important to her than her own son.

"It wasn't like that. Mom only wanted to help An-ling because she was going to be a great painter. Then Mom and Dad started having some problems. Older people, you know, everything becomes a big deal with them. Mom and Dad argued a lot, over what to eat for dinner, what movie to see, where to go on vacation. Mom needed some time off, that's all. She didn't leave to *be* with An-ling.

"And it wasn't a big deal. I knew she was going to come back and so did Dad. It's happened to a lot of the kids in my class, except most of their parents get divorced. Mom came back."

Sergeant Daniel finally did sit down on a bench. "Set your butt down here too. Scottie needs a rest." I sat down at the other end.

"How many times did you go to Brooklyn, to the studio?"

I wanted to lie again, but his face had turned real serious. He wasn't going to take any bullshit.

"Four or five times maybe, but I only went there to see my mother."

"I thought you only saw your mother for brunch on Sundays in Manhattan?"

"Sometimes I wanted to see her more."

"Nate! Nate!" Beanpole was running down the path. He was waving his arm, his hand flapping in front of his face like a screw in his wrist had come loose. "He's home." My heart started pounding. Glad for the interruption, panicked at what was to come.

By the time we made it back up to Riverside Drive, Mom had come home too. Dad started arguing with Sergeant Daniel. Mom wanted me to go to Mrs. Ricklin's and stay there. The two men with the satchels headed first for my parents' bedroom. Dad tried to follow, but Sergeant Daniel blocked the door.

"Why don't the three of you wait in the living room? Let us get our work done and we'll be out of here in no time."

Dad didn't budge. "What kind of idiot judge issued this search warrant? On what grounds? You're looking for what? This makes no sense! No goddamn sense! You're going to take her clothes, her letters, her makeup? What else? Her laptop? You're going to find nothing and then what? The innocent citizen grins and bears it. Is that it? You can't really think my wife had anything to do with this, Sergeant. In Fort Greene, just the other day, ten blocks from where the girl lived, some druggie shot three people dead."

I kept looking at Mom, who hadn't moved from the front door. I wanted her to tell Dad to shut up. Her eyes kept sliding from Dad to Sergeant Daniel, but her mouth stayed tight.

"Did you ask the druggie about An-ling, Sergeant Daniel? How do you know he didn't kill her too? Did you get a search warrant, invade his home, go through his clothes? No, right? Because you blacks stick together. A white middle-class woman, she's a killer for sure. I know what you're doing. Don't think I don't. You're getting back at us for—"

I flung my arms around his chest, hugged him hard. "Dad. Please, Dad. Just let them get through with it." He put his arms on my shoulders real slow, and he started breathing again. I could feel his heart beating hard against my cheek. "It'll be okay, Dad."

The three of us sat in the living room after that. Forty-five minutes later the police were gone. They took some of Mom's clothes and all three of our laptops.

The next morning Sergeant Daniel's testimony for the prosecution continues. In his hands he holds two sworn statements dated April 27, 2005 and May 17, 2005, both signed by Emma Perotti. They have been entered into evidence as People's Exhibits Two and Three.

"Sergeant Daniel, in your May seventeenth meeting with Mrs. Perotti, did you repeat some of the questions you asked in your April twenty-seventh meeting with the defendant?"

"Yes, I did."

Guzman, his arms folded, rocks gently on his heels. "How did Mrs. Perotti answer the repeated questions?"

"She varied her answer in one instance."

"Please explain to the jury."

"On April twenty-seventh I asked the defendant when she had last been in the Tercer Street loft and she stated that she left the loft on March thirtieth and never went back. When I asked the same question on May seventeenth, she stated that she went back to the loft on April seventeenth."

"Did you ask her why she lied in her first statement?"

Fishkin leaps up. "Objection!"

"Withdrawn. Do you know why the defendant changed her statement?"

"She stated she'd put the April seventeenth visit out of her mind because she was so upset about her friend's death, and it was only after I showed her the hardware store owner's statement that she remembered."

"Did you ask her why she went back to the loft on April seventeenth?"

"I did. She stated that she needed to pick up some clothes she'd forgotten."

"Did you ask the defendant to explain why she bought the can of insulation foam on that day?"

"Yes."

"Please read to the jury her answer from the May seventeenth statement."

Sergeant Daniel fishes a pair of glasses from his breast pocket. After a quick glance at Emma Perotti, he slips them on.

"'The last time I visited the loft, on April seventeenth'"—his voice is soft, but naturally low enough to carry across the courtroom—"a mouse ran out from under the kitchen sink. I grabbed a broom to kill it, but it got away. An-ling was scared of mice and when I found a large hole under the sink, I went down to the hardware store a few blocks away, bought a can of insulation foam, came back to the loft and plugged the hole.'"

"Thank you, Sergeant." Guzman walks back to his table and picks up a clear plastic bag containing what looks like a white item of clothing. He gives it to a court officer. "Your Honor, at this point I would like to offer People's Exhibit Eight into evidence."

After the court reporter has labeled the exhibit, a court officer takes it to Sergeant Daniel.

"Please remove it from the bag, Sergeant," Guzman says. "Show it to the jury."

Daniel draws the item out, unfolds it with great care and holds it over the railing of the witness stand. It's a very wrinkled embroidered silk blouse.

"Sergeant Daniel, can you identify that blouse and how it came to be in police custody?"

"Yes. On April twenty-sixth, me and three of my men went to the defendant's home with a search warrant. I found the shirt in the defendant's closet. It had her laundry mark on the label at the back of the collar: 'EP.'"

"Did you take all of the defendant's clothing into police custody?"

"No."

"Why did you take this blouse in particular?"

"We found it stuffed in a straw handbag at the back of the closet."

"No further questions."

Subj: Fairytales and fantasies
Date: 04-09-05 19:42:12 EST
From: Chinesecanary@BetterLateThan Never.com
To: EPerotti@aol.com

The time when you were on the phone with your school for a long time—it was my next visit after Josh told me about Amy—I went to your bedroom and looked through your closet, the drawers of your bedside table. I wanted to find evidence of her. A photo, a stuffed toy, a pair of shoes, something that would tell me Amy had existed. I found nothing.

I went to Mapleton. The Catholic cemetery was near the railroad tracks, a five-minute walk from the train station. I found Amy's tomb next to a white hydrangea bush, a small stone on the ground. Carved underneath a cross: Amy Celestina Howells, April 10, 1987–October 21, 1989.

Nothing else.

The stone was dirty, the corners covered in moss. No flowers, just the bush, which I decided you had planted for her. I sat down next to her grave and wondered what it's like for the dead to hear the trains coming and going, footsteps on the path beside them, the sound of the wind in the trees. Do they like the company of the living world, or are the dead angry they have been taken away from jobs not completed? Cleaning out the attic, writing the report, finishing the coloring book, healing the sick child. Do they know who visits them, who doesn't? Do they give good fortune to those who come, seek vengeance on those who stay away? I wish I knew.

The dirt on the stone told me no one visited Amy. I cleaned and crushed pages of my sketchbook into mourning flowers which I circled around her name. In the bottom of my pocket I found two candies— lemon and grape, covered in lint and bits of tobacco. I cleaned them as best I could and left them, one on each side of the dates, so that the beginning and the end are sweet.

The library was far, almost an hour's walk from the cemetery. Curiosity carried me.

Why did you, who have been so kind and generous to me, not write anything on the tomb? Why don't you bring new flowers every week?

When you lost her, was the grief too much to hold inside a few black lines? Is your heart so strong it can keep such pain to itself? These are the things I wondered as I walked.

The death announcement, I wanted to glean it for traces of your feel- ings. I had the death date, I asked for copies of the local newspaper from that week.

Looking for the death announcement, I found the article. Amy's death brought shame on you, the way my birth brought shame on my mother.

A-l

EIGHT

Emma

ABOVE THE DOWNWARD slope of converted factories and warehouses, the Manhattan Bridge arched blue. Below, jade green in the sun, a swath of the East River. In front of the window I had just cleaned, a fist of paper towel still in my hand, I watched, listened as, on the lower level of the bridge, the train from Manhattan rumbled past the window. I wondered if this was the one An-ling was on, whether she was, at this moment, walking toward this studio.

I'd been waiting in the hot, light-drenched loft for more than an hour.

"I got lost," An-ling offered, blinking at the brightness of the room from the doorway. In her wrinkled black T-shirt and jeans, she looked no older than Josh. A hot pink plastic satchel hung from a drooping shoulder. Her hair was dirty, uncombed. She looked sullen, put-out to be dragged all the way to Brooklyn from midtown and the Art Students League.

"I got off at the wrong stop." Her hand clutched the door jamb. She didn't want this place, a small Brooklyn loft in an area known as DUMBO, which stands for Down Under the Manhattan Bridge Overpass. I was the one insisting she take a look at it. At least she'd come. No commitment, no strings attached, I'd promised. Only a simple look at what could be hers for a while. The place belonged to a colleague of mine who had moved to Arizona but hadn't decided whether to sell it or not. She was letting me have it until June for the price of the maintenance, which was affordable if I was careful. An-ling belonged here, in a clean, airy space filled with light, in a neighborhood of other artists. I saw her blooming here.

I took her arm and pulled her across the concrete floor on which the previous artists had marked their passage with rainbow streaks, swirls, sprinkles of paint. High above us, a patterned tin ceiling held spools of rust.

"They once manufactured bolts and nails in this building," I said. An-ling remained silent as I walked her along the brick wall covered in a thick crust of white paint. At the center window I watched her take in the view.

"The subway makes a lot of noise and you can barely see the river," I said. "The ceiling is rusty; the shower leaks; the oven door doesn't close properly and this floor is a mess and very hard on your feet." I was taking my cue from Chinese mothers, who, according to An-ling, showered their newborns with insults—

ugly, wicked, piglet, toad—to confuse the evil spirits. I pointed out defects to confuse An-ling into accepting.

She turned her back to the window and slid down to the floor. A hand, small, with tidy oval nails that reminded me of translucent shells, dug through the contents of her hot pink satchel. "I'm going native again." She held up a box of hair dye, her sullenness replaced by a defiance I didn't understand.

I sat down beside her. "Want my help?"

"How much does it cost?"

"My help? Nothing."

"The place." She was looking at the expanse of wall next to the cooking area. It was the only wall in shadow. "That's the place to paint. Too much light flattens everything and you can't see true color. A northern exposure is best."

"We'll put up blinds."

She turned to me so that our faces were only inches apart. There was pride in her eyes. "If I accept, what will it cost?"

"I told you not to worry about rent. It belongs to a friend of mine. It will cost me practically nothing."

She raised a sceptical eyebrow. "I'll never be able to pay you back."

"Payback will be to see you thrive, develop your talent, be happy."

She inched closer. I could smell the oil paint on her, the cigarettes. "Why do you want to help me? What have I done for you that you're so generous? What do you get out of this?"

"You're a special young lady with a great deal of talent and I'd like to help foster that talent."

"Maybe you are like the fox who can change into many forms. Ghosts ride on a fox. Demons take the shape of a fox. After dark the fox can turn into a human to tempt you. You don't act like the other people I know. I don't know what to expect from you."

"Why don't you trust me? I'm your friend."

"There's a price to pay for everything we do, everything we accept from others. Maybe now you think there's no price, but later it'll show itself clear in your head, and I won't be able to pay."

What price had been asked of her in the past? She had received so little from life. "No price."

"Have you done this before?"

"No."

"You must know a lot of students who need help."

"Look, you can't put my intentions on trial, okay? If you don't want the studio, fine, don't take it." I started to get up. My sandal slipped on the floor and I fell back against the wall. The intensity of her distrust was unbearable.

"There's only one me," I said. "No shape-changing."

Her eyes widened. "I remind you of someone. That's it, isn't it? That's why you're so good to me."

She waited. What was the risk of telling her?

"Lady Teachers must always tell the truth."

I hadn't told Josh; how could I tell her? "There *is* someone you remind me of, but it's only one of the reasons I like you."

"From China?"

"No, American. White. You don't look at all alike. That is, she died as a little girl, so I don't know how she would have looked. Something about you brings her back. I can't explain it better than that."

"Who was she?"

"A friend's child." Amy's death stayed inside me, as deep as the bones in her grave. "She was killed in a car accident, many years ago."

An-ling's cheek touched mine. "I've always wanted a sister. A little girl to play with."

I fumbled to my feet. "What about the studio? Do you want it? I have to give an answer today."

An-ling nodded.

"Wonderful!" I kissed the top of her head.

She caught my hands. "But wait! I must pay you back. I have no money now, but later when I am a better painter you can choose the best ones. It's a deal?"

"A deal." She let go of me. "You're a tough woman to convince. What should we do to celebrate?"

"No celebration. It will bring bad luck."

"Come on, An-ling. You're in the United States now. Your evil spirits have no power here."

"Maybe. Maybe not." She walked over to the wall in shadow and flattened her back against it. "Portrait of the artist as a young woman."

Looking at her, at the happiness she now let play on her face, I understood that it wasn't Amy that she brought back into my life. It was the memory of maternal love, all-enveloping, never-ending, which I had assumed was going to carry me across the countries of my life as lightly as a balloon. A love free of loss. A love I had vowed to keep hidden from my son.

"An-ling, I want to celebrate."

"This new home is enough for me." Her expression turned serious, concentrated, as though she were taking the measure of me. "I will pay you back with a secret." She held up her wrists, quickly unhooked the beaded bracelets. They fell to the floor with a soft swish. An-ling turned her palms upward, offered me the view of two clean scars on her wrists. "A stupid moment. I'm happy now I did not go deep."

Her confession moved me. "I'm happy too. Promise me you will never try it again. Please!"

She buttoned the bracelets back on. "You will stay with me sometimes here? We'll cook together and eat and then you will sit in the corner in a big chair, reading while I paint. Say you will. Please!"

"I have a family, An-ling."

She turned slowly, taking in the expanse of the room. "Sometimes at night I think I'm underwater and no one can see me or hear me and I'll drown."

"I'm here." I held her. "We'll buy a guest futon."

At the sight of An-ling's scarred wrists, my mind spiraled back to a mid-June morning, eight months after Amy died. Tom was back at work. Lucy, the woman he had hired to help me, was in the basement doing a load of laundry. She was supposed to watch me, but she preferred dealing with the housework.

After the laundry, Lucy ironed, and I had given her enough shirts to keep her in the basement for a long time. While the water was running in the bathtub, I opened the medicine chest where Tom kept a box of old-fashioned razorblades to pare down his corns. I unwrapped a new blade and thought of all the blood I was going to lose, how Tom was going to hate the mess, how Lucy might be proud of her clean-up job. I undressed and lowered myself into the bathtub. Turning my left wrist, I followed the meanderings of my veins until they disappeared in the cushion of my palm. I ran the razor across the white skin, just below the hand. A shallow cut, a trial run. Blood beaded in a line, started to drip. The last time I had taken a bath—Amy had been dead only a few days—Tom had lowered me into the tub, washed me with great care. I had lain there wishing he'd let go of me, let me slip down underwater. A rivulet of menstrual blood twisted out from between my legs. I watched it float, fade into the water and vowed to myself I would never get pregnant again. Tom plugged me up with a sponge while I howled.

Now I looked at my bloodied wrist. My period. A wave of panic overwhelmed me. When was the last time? Not last month. Two months? Three? How long had it been? God, how long? I wrapped my wrist in a towel, scrambled out of the bathtub, showered it down to remove any trace of blood. Tom's blade, cleaned, dried, went into its box. My suicide? Postponed.

Five drugstore pregnancy tests later, I accepted the truth. I was pregnant.

I had only three clear thoughts: I do not deserve the joy of another baby. I will suffer her death. Then I will kill myself. Such is the solipsism of grief.

Three days before my appointment with the abortion clinic, I dreamed of Amy as she was the morning she died, dressed in a yellow T-shirt, blue shorts, a pink barrette clipped in her hair. She curled inside me, a two-year-old fetus. Then she was gone, replaced by a baby whose face and sex I couldn't make out. I woke up feeling the baby's weight pushing against the wall of my uterus. Only a two-month fetus, not more than a cluster of cells, and yet her weight stayed with me throughout the day and when night came again I lay in bed, imagining this new baby pushing itself out of me, crawling, still attached to me, up the hill of my stomach, to reach my breast. The baby sucks while I clean her, cover her with my nightgown, hold her. With that image I fell asleep.

The next morning I took the train to Grand Central Station and walked the eleven blocks to the best of God's New York mansions—St. Patrick's Cathedral, my grandmother's favorite. I knelt in the front pew and listened to the silence, waited for the comfort of belief to envelop me like the blanket Nonna used to fold over me when we went to sleep at night.

I could feel Nonna's presence in that church, watching me, waiting to see if I measured up, if I would disappoint her. She never got over the trauma of being dragged to America, away from her village, her parents and friends. She never overcame the shame of not giving birth to a son, of having a rebellious, bawdy woman for her only child. Nonna was stern, unforgiving, and yet she opened her home to her renegade daughter and a bastard grandchild. She took me into her bed, scolded me, fed me, made sure I went out into the world scrubbed to a sheen and wearing clean, pressed clothes. She was, in her words, the whalebones of my life's corset.

I hated sleeping in the double bed Nonna had shared with her husband, dead years before I was born. Nonna snored. As she got older she smelled acrid. But my only other choice was the sofabed in the living room with my mother. I stayed with Nonna. As I grew older, I began to love the room, its quiet, the darkness of it—Nonna never pulled up the shade, too proud to let prying neighbors see how plain, how poor her bedroom was. That room was my retreat from my mother, from the neighborhood kids who called her a whore and me a bastard. The scent of the candle Nonna kept burning on a makeshift altar next to the bed started to smell as good as the fried dough she made on holidays. When she woke up and before going to sleep, Nonna would kneel in front of the candle, cross herself with her rosary and pray to the pictures of her parents and the Madonna propped on the altar. Even now, if I try to picture God, I see my great-grandfather's mustached face, his eyebrows so thick and long the ends curl up.

It was the serene, stilled expression on Nonna's face as she prayed that mesmerized me, that made me want to believe as she did. She was overjoyed when I asked her to make me into a good Catholic. She led me to believe that my submission to God would bring not happiness, because that was not our lot in life, but a sense of security, a feeling of being loved back by Jesus, the Virgin Mary and all the saints. God and his vast family, Nonna promised, would take care of me and mine.

Sitting in the front pew of St. Patrick's, pregnant, I tried to rekindle my belief in God with the spark of memory. How comfortable I had once felt sitting in church, surrounded by the damp smell of wet winter coats, the shuffling feet, intermittent coughs, the creaks of the pew as we knelt, the unfurling veil of incense.

Nonna's voice slid into my ears, speaking the words she repeated at every sight of a crucified Christ. "When you feel sorry for yourself, think of the pain He must have gone through to sacrifice His only son."

I crossed myself, a gesture I had foresworn after Amy's death, and spoke to God.

"Watch over this baby. Keep her safe from me and whoever and whatever else could harm her. I will live to take care of her, but I will love her in silence. Silence is my penance for Amy."

I wasn't foolish enough to wait for a sign of His agreement. On the train back to Mapleton, watching the rain dash against the window, I began to doubt the sincerity of my sudden, convenient reconversion. God as an excuse for wanting to live, wanting to have this baby, an excuse to relieve my guilt. I wondered if it was God I had worshiped all those years or Nonna, rigid with certainties, self-righteous, constant, with her stringent rules, what she called "the rungs on the ladder to heaven." Nonna, even with her cruelties, the whalebones in my corset. A woman I loved deeply.

Many hours later, I opened the front door. Tom's shoulders were covered with sparkles where the porch light fell on the raindrops of his slicker. His face held only hurt and

incomprehension. The sight of him filled me with a tenderness I had forgotten. I wrapped my arms around him, pulled
him inside the house.

"We're still together," I said. "A threesome. A family.
Forgive me." We began crying with relief, with love.

In the dark, with Tom spooned against me, his hand pro-
tective, possessive, on my belly, I said, "Promise me you'll
keep our baby safe."

I accepted my new pregnancy, but I still shunned company—
everyone acting cheerful, crowding my days with brain-
numbing activities, stuffing me with suggestions on how to
go on with my life, take it in stride, make peace with it, look
for solace in God, in the gym, in work, in the mall. Telling
me to consider myself blessed because I was pregnant again.
Their intrusions, delivered without looking at me, their eyes
safe from my killer face, made me angry. They never mentioned their own children and I imagined them, as soon as
I was gone, chanting a litany of their names to ward off the
evil eye I'd become.

I was relieved that our baby was a boy, that our new child
would not compete with the memory of Amy, but I couldn't
bear to put him in her room. It was still filled with her soft
snore, her waking gurgles, sounds I heard in the night,
amplified, as though her monitor were still on. Josh slept in
the den.

My love for Josh was instantly there, lodged in my bones,
but in St. Patick's I had renounced the joy of rocking him
in my arms, feeling his warmth, smelling his softness. I
became an efficient mother. I kept him fed, clean, warm. At

times I stole a quick hug, skated my hand over his cheek, let his hair brush my lips. As he grew so did my love until it pounded against my chest, but I was too scared to release it, to show it openly, to break my pact. What if I should lose him too?

Guilt had made me so self-absorbed I never stopped to think what I was doing to my son, how I was depriving him of what was his right. Filled with envy, I watched Tom as he stepped in to fill the gaps. Tom, who slowly edged me out of the parenting game until I was rendered useless.

I would squint at Josh and try to remember what Amy had looked like. Tom had destroyed the photos, the videos. Sleeping on the first day of her life, her first birthday, first steps, first ball thrown—actions repeated by every healthy child. Remarkable only because it is your child. Now lost. Josh looked nothing like her.

Tom

At the end of July, I was finishing teaching a summer-school course. An-ling came into my office one afternoon without knocking.

"You had a daughter," she said immediately, "and you let her run out of the house and Emma ran over her. Then what? A couple of months later you two made another one, like babies are interchangeable, supermarket products? A can of coffee runs out; buy another one!" She started to cry.

"It was an accident and a long time ago." I did not invite her to sit down. It was none of her business and I mistrusted her tears. There was no reason for them that I could understand, not from what I knew of her at the time. "I'm expecting a student any minute."

She turned her back to me before I had even finished, which surprised me as I didn't expect to be rid of her so easily. From the way she had planted herself in our kitchen almost every afternoon until I had put a stop to it, she'd struck me as a single-minded girl, not easily discouraged.

"Wait a minute," I said.

She stopped, not turning around, wanting me to admire how good her ass looked in those tight slacks, how smooth and inviting her bare back was.

"How did you find out?"

She turned then, pulled at the straw that was her hair. She wiped her face with the back of her hand. I asked her to sit down.

She poured herself into the chair in one fluid motion, wrapping one tightly bound leg over the other. I have seen female students in my classes make similar moves when they are sitting next to a male they want to entice.

"How did you find out?" I asked again, making a show of looking at my watch.

"Emma and I tell each other everything."

I would have liked to slap her. "You're lying."

When Emma and I left Westchester for the city—Josh was two at the time—we shed our old life, my job, our friends. New York was to be a fresh start for us. I insisted that we shouldn't tell people about Amy. For the outside world,

Josh included, she had never existed. I wanted to give Emma a chance to fully turn to Josh. I wanted, above all, for Josh to be free and clear of the weight of Amy's death. For all of us to be free of it.

Among other things, I teach game theory, the study of how rational individuals make decisions when they're interdependent. It's a way of calculating risk. There's a game I teach my first-year students called the Prisoner's Dilemma. The police have arrested two thieves who are both guilty, but there isn't sufficient proof to convict them. Each prisoner, separated from the other, with no contact possible, is offered a choice. If he pleads guilty, he'll go to jail for a month on a misdemeanor charge. If he pleads innocent and is found guilty, he can go to jail for six months, but if his colleague pleads innocent and is also found guilty, they will both go to jail for three months. All three choices carry a cost. The point is to calculate which choice will have the least cost.

Emma and I chose what we thought, what I was convinced, was the least costly of solutions, and I was satisfied that silence had paid off. In my mind we had become a sound, viable family, with Amy's death in the past, its rightful place.

"Why did you come here and tell me what I already know? What's your point? Let me make it perfectly clear to you that what goes on in my family, past, present and future, is none of your business and never will be if I can help it." I stood up and walked to the door. As I passed her I picked up her scent—something cheap, flowery, mixed in with the smell of smoke.

"Please go."

She stayed right where she was, simply pivoting her bare shoulders so that she could keep her half-masked eyes on me. Her expression was stolid. "You don't like me and I think maybe you're scared of me. I don't know why. I like Emma and I like you and Josh. You're a nice family. Why can't you be nice to me? That's all I want, people to be nice." She reached down to pick up her bag, a pink plastic thing. Her top drooped open; I could see clear to her navel. She had no breasts to speak of.

I left her sitting in my office. When I came back, maybe fifteen minutes later, she had left a note.

"I'm sorry about your daughter. That is what I came to tell you."

It was another one of her lies.

I turned the air-conditioner on high to remove any trace of her smell, locked the door and, sitting at my desk, waited for my anger to subside.

What Emma had done was unforgivable. She had broken our pact of silence, shared our tragedy with a conniving young girl who should never have been allowed to walk into our lives. Now this girl knew. My biggest fear was that she would tell Josh.

My son found out about his sister from the tabloids. He says it's all right, that he understands why I never told him. It's hard to believe him and my heart cries for him, for how I've disappointed him. I keep wishing like a child: Why doesn't life furnish us with a playback button?

Subj: Fairytales and fantasies
Date: 04-09-05 20:21:55 EST
From: Chinesecanary@BetterLateThanNever.com
To: EPerotti@aol.com

"A translation remains a substitute, lacking the wholeness of the original." The painter Fairfield Porter wrote that.

I am not a translation. That's what I wanted to say, sitting on the floor in the loft that first day. I'm not a reflection, a shadow, a substitute. I have my own heart, bones, meat, skin. I am me. An original.

Amy is dead, in a coffin, underground. If you want her, go to the Mapleton Catholic Cemetery. She's in row nine by the hydrangea plant. She's probably still waiting for you. Daughters hang on a long time after they've been abandoned.

If you want to do things for me, I appreciate it, but do them for me, not in her memory. That's what I wanted to say, but I didn't because I wanted you and your family and the loft.

Do you want to see your daughter again? On a swing, kicking up dead leaves, smearing chocolate birthday cake over her face, sitting on your lap with the devil's eyes from the camera flash?

If you call me I'll tell you where she is. I can give Amy back to you. Her image at least.

Call me please.

A-I

NINE

TRACY GORMAN IS a thin, short-haired blonde woman in her early-thirties, wearing a navy suit and red-framed glasses. She has been a police lab technician for four years. In her hands she holds Emma Perotti's silk embroidered blouse.

"Did you examine that blouse under a microscope?" asks Guzman.

"I did."

"Please tell the jury what you found."

"The first thing I found was traces of eyeliner and blush high on the left sleeve of the blouse and also on the left shoulder. I ran a test comparing the eyeliner and blush with the ones found in Miss Huang's bathroom. They matched. That led me back to the body. Someone had carefully cleaned Miss Huang's face with soap, Dove soap in fact, but I was able to find traces of the same make-up."

"Is that all you found?"

"No." Gorman holds up the blouse against her chest with one hand and loops her other hand over the embroidery pattern. "In the silk threads of the flowers, I found particles of a white substance that I was later able to identify as insulation foam."

"Did you examine those particles for any DNA?"

"I did."

"What did you find?"

"A few of the particles found on the blouse had traces of An-ling Huang's saliva."

Emma

An-ling, wrapped in a towel, sat on a stool in front of my bathroom mirror while I sheathed my hands in plastic gloves and straightened out the damp hair clotted on her head. She had asked me to dye her hair back to black. Around us the apartment was silent except for the occasional diminished rumble of Saturday traffic from Riverside Drive. Tom and Josh were rafting on the Delaware River and wouldn't be back until late afternoon.

As I combed her hair she bent over the sink. Her towel swooped down to reveal the curve of her buttocks. Between dimples I saw a dark blue mark.

"Did you hurt yourself? You have a nasty bruise."

She laughed. "That's a tattoo."

"Oh." I squinted down and made out a boat, a junk with blue sails.

"You don't like it."

"I don't like having weak eyes. The tattoo is pretty."

"When I was little," An-ling said, "my back was covered with dark marks. A lot of Chinese children have these Mongolian spots. I used to scrub my back very hard to make them go away. They made me feel dirty."

"You have a clear back now." I combed the dye through her hair, piled it high on top of her head and set the timer to fifteen minutes. "Why are they called Mongolian spots?"

"When the Mongols invaded China, back in the early times, they killed the men, raped the women, made our children slaves. Ever since, we carry these marks to remind us. Women and men both. We are together, for once, in this ancient shame. But the marks stay only for a short while . . . until the third or fourth year. Do you think shame can go away after so little time?" In the mirror, her stare was bright, intense.

"I think it would depend on the reason for the shame."

"Lying brings shame." An-ling swiveled on her stool until she faced me, naked except for her towel now on her lap. She had strong shoulders, muscled arms and the jutting hips of a woman, but her breasts were shallow curves, timid rises of skin, her nipples tucked, still in hiding. She was ambiguous, neither woman nor child. Confused by her words, by her nakedness, I wanted to hug her, cover her with renewed tenderness.

"Aren't you cold?" I reached for a towel on the rack and draped it over her shoulders.

"There are lies to become rich, to be famous, or to make believe you are both. Those are stupid lies. And there are lies as necessary as air. They only help you breathe, nothing more. Those lies are good. Do you agree, Lady Teacher?"

How did she know about such things? She was so young; how did she know?

"Lies are never good." The timer showed four minutes left before the dye needed to be rinsed out. "At the studio the other day I said you reminded me of someone . . ." Could I explain to An-ling the bile of guilt I'd been carrying with me all these years and how being with her, helping her, was overwhelmingly sweet?

Before I could say more, An-ling took my hands and pushed them lightly against my breasts, gone soft with age. "You're so big," she said.

Her gesture startled me out of my confessional mood. I stepped back. "Southern Italian genes. I had nothing to do with it. In fact, I always dreamed of being a B cup. I was twelve years old when the boys in school nicknamed me Emma-moo. I didn't like that one bit."

"I bet they all wanted to fuck you."

"If they did I never noticed." The timer went off and I turned the shower on. "Be sure to rinse until the water runs clear. I'll be in the kitchen."

An-ling stood in front of the mirror, the towel now on the floor. "I hate my breasts!" The dye started trickling down her forehead. "Pancakes, pennies, fried eggs. God, I'm ugly!"

"You are beautiful, An-ling. Really, you are." I swept my thumb across her forehead before the dye reached her eyes. "Many men will love you. You'll have to push them away, they'll be so many."

"Do you love me?"

"Yes, I do. Very much."

"You love me not just because I remind you of someone? You love me, An-ling Nai Huang, flat-chested crazy girl from Su-kai in district of Xin-hui?"

I turned her around to face me and cupped her chin. "Of course I do. I love An-ling Nai Huang, beautiful young girl from Su-kai in the district of Xin-hui." She laughed, a little girl made happy so easily. And then she threw her arms around my neck and kissed me, a soft sweet kiss on the lips, a kiss Amy and I had shared countless times.

I drew back, ready to tell her to get in the shower. In the mirror, Tom and Josh stared at us.

I registered disgust on Tom's face.

Tom

We stood in that bathroom doorway no more than twenty, thirty seconds. Then I took hold of my son, pushed him away, out of the apartment, down to the park. We followed the river, made a pretense of looking at the sailboats. It was a clear August day with a breeze keeping the New York humidity under control. A perfect day to go rafting. I cursed myself for getting sick, throwing up on the raft, which was the reason we had come back so early.

I couldn't find any words to explain, to defuse what Josh had seen. My son had just witnessed his mother kissing that naked girl and no paternal power could change that, no matter how much I wanted to. How could she? In our home?

The muscles of my arms still burned with the desire to slap Emma, to hit them both, kick them out on the street. I have never considered violence a part of my makeup, but what I saw in that bathroom was so repulsive, so hurtful, so sudden, that I had no defenses ready. I needed to strike out, would have if I hadn't leaned back and felt Josh's shoulder against my back in the doorway. My thirteen-year-old son was seeing what I saw. I grabbed his arm so hard I left a bruise.

"Women like to play together," I ended up saying. "They put on makeup, try on clothes and tell each other how fat or skinny they are."

"Then why can't we go home and you get to bed?"

"I'm sure they're embarrassed being caught like that, An-ling half-naked."

"Totally naked."

"All the more reason to give her time to get dressed and leave. There was nothing in it. Just two girls playing."

"Yeah, pretty dumb, I guess."

"Some of them never really grow up."

I threw up in the bushes. Josh loped off to buy me a soda from a street vender.

In the weeks that followed, I convinced myself I had finally knocked my face against the ugly truth of my wife's relationship with that girl. At night, lying in bed next to Emma, my mind would replay the scene over and over. The girl naked, Emma fully dressed. If I hadn't walked in at that precise moment, what else would Emma have done with her? My wife's hands, where were they? I tried to find them in my memory of those thirty seconds, but all I could conjure up was the girl's expanse of skin shining under the light, in the mirror, close enough to touch, her arms around my wife, Emma's lips clamped on hers.

I couldn't stop thinking about that sight. I, who had always prided myself in understanding my wife and my son. I, who strove to be one step ahead of their thoughts, to better protect, take care of them. God damn it! That is a husband's, a father's role in life. How did I fail so miserably?

My failure fueled my disgust.

Sitting in this courtroom, I live with the threat that I will lose what I have fought hard to keep whole. I am still revolted, and enraged. At myself this time.

If only that girl had never showed up in our kitchen. If only Emma had behaved responsibly. If only I had kept a better watch on Josh.

If only. The emotions unleashed by those two words could power the greatest storms on earth.

Josh

She's gorgeous! That's what came to my head first. Her body—it was something special, something to keep looking at—made me forget anything else. Her skin looked like you could bite into it, and the taste was going to be like whipped cream slipping down your tongue. Touching her that time in the basement—I could feel it in my hands again, how soft and warm she was. In the bathroom, seeing all of her, my heart bounced, became a big fat ball against my lungs. I didn't breathe, afraid it would burst.

It took me a few seconds to see she and Mom were kissing.

In the park, Dad looked like he'd run into a wall and I didn't know what to do except tell him he should go home and lie down. I told him I was going to forget the whole thing, but I knew An-ling's body was going to stay front and center in my head. The rest, it was just kissing. I mean, it wasn't this earth-shaking event; it wasn't going to turn our lives around.

When Dad threw up, I ran to get him a soda. He got teary and told me I was a good son. He was so totally grateful it made me nauseous too.

That night, thinking about An-ling gave me a hard-on.

Emma

Only sounds. The click of the bathroom door shut in our faces. The slam of the front door trailed by the ringing of the sleigh bells on the knob. An-ling's startled breaths.

Streaming hot water from the shower clouded the bathroom with steam. I had done nothing shameful, and yet I knew that something had been broken between Tom and me. The look on his face told me that much.

"I'm sorry," An-ling said. She looked embarrassed. "I didn't mean anything—"

"It'll be fine. You better rinse your hair out or it'll fall off."

"Do you want me to explain to Tom?"

It would only make it worse. "There's nothing to explain, An-ling. Go, get in."

She stepped in and closed the shower door behind her, becoming a blur.

Now I wonder if the downward turn of An-ling's life can be pinpointed to the moment when Josh and Tom walked in and saw us.

"Are you going to give her up?" Tom and I were in bed after a miserable family evening in a restaurant.

"Give her up? What do you mean? She's not a drug habit."

"Isn't she?"

"She's someone I care about." The words came out fuzzy. I'd drunk too much wine at dinner. "Someone I want to help, that's all."

"Kissing her, that's helping."

"You have a nasty mind."

"Me? You're the dyke."

That word wrapped itself around me, layer upon layer of implication tightening, leaving me unable to breathe. It took me minutes to answer. I wanted to shout but had to whisper for Josh's sake. His bedroom abuts ours.

"We've been married a very long time, Tom. We've made love too many times to count. And the word is lesbian."

"I saw what I saw."

"I can't believe you're saying this."

"Believe it."

"Want me to prove I'm not a dyke?" My hand closed over his penis and started to pump. Tom jerked me away. "I'm sorry you didn't get the chairmanship, Tom. But you can't take your rage out on me."

"Rage?"

"Yes, rage." I squeezed my eyes shut to hold back tears. "We did nothing wrong."

He grabbed my shoulders and pressed his fingers against the bones. "I don't want you to see her again."

I punched him in the stomach, once, twice. He let go of me. "She could be our daughter, Tom."

"Like hell she could."

"An-ling is alone. She wants a family. What's wrong with that?"

"Not my family."

"It's not only yours. It's my family and Josh's too. We get an equal vote. Josh likes her. I'm not asking for her to move in. I just want her to be in our life. At least in mine."

"Why did you tell her about Amy?"

Tom's words chilled my heart. "What are you talking about?"

"That little bitch came to my office, said she knew all about Amy. You told her."

"I didn't tell her anything."

"That's why we moved to New York, remember? So that Josh would never know. What if she tells him? What's he going to think of us? Answer me that. What is your son going to think?"

"I didn't tell her."

"Then how did she find out?"

"I have no idea. She won't tell Josh if I ask her. She's a sweet girl. If you don't trust her, at least trust me."

Tom pushed himself under the covers. "I don't want you to ever see her again." He turned his back to me. For him, the matter was settled.

"No!" My reserve of strength surprised me. "You can't punish me this time. There are no toys or photographs to burn, no bedroom to strip of every last trace of her. I won't give her up because this time I'm not guilty of anything, Tom. I've done nothing wrong. All these years you've blamed me for Amy's death."

He sat up. "You blamed yourself, Emma." His face hardened. "It's either us or her."

"I won't let you do this to me. Not this time." I switched off my light, turned my back to him and in the silence that followed, dropped into a wine-heavy sleep.

Sometime in the night, I woke up, ugly thoughts sliming my tongue along with the evening's wine. I could hear Tom throwing up in the bathroom. I got up and handed him a glass of water. "Is it me or what you didn't eat?"

"Hell, I have the stomach flu." I almost admired his will to take us out to dinner, to sit with the smell of food under his nose, all of it to show Josh we were a sitcom family. Only the laugh track was missing. I couldn't bring myself to actually feel anything except a steady burn, as though my insides had been grated down.

"Do you want to fuck her? Is that why you think my kissing her lips means I'm having sex with her? You're hot for her. That's why you don't want her around, isn't it? Keep temptation at bay?"

"Don't try to twist this thing around, Emma. It won't work. You're the one who wants her, not me. And if Josh finds out about Amy, God help me, Emma—" He gagged, dropped his head over the toilet bowl. He had nothing left to throw up.

"Maybe it's time he did find out." I walked out.

Subj: Fairytales and fantasies
Date: 04-10-05 22:20:04 EST
From: Chinesecanary@BetterLateThanNever.com
To: EPerotti@aol.com

I ask you to call me but I don't send my e-mails. I store them for
when? I don't know. For when the courage of the tiger comes to me.
For when I'm far away.

How can I send you what I don't want you to know, the real shame of
my life? It has nothing to do with Mongols.

:-(An-ling

TEN

Josh

A STEADY KNOCK against my bed's head-
board followed by, "Time to get your drum beat going."
Dad's corny way to wake me up on a school day.

"It's Sunday!" I buried my head under the pillow.

"Get up, son. Pack your duffle bag. Shorts, T-shirts,
bathing suits. Don't forget underwear."

Why was Dad rushing me out of bed on a Sunday? Then
I remembered An-ling naked in the bathroom the day
before. I woke up real fast once my brain booted up that
fact. Dad was digging in my drawers and throwing my stuff
on the bed. He was fully dressed. Sundays he's usually in his
bathrobe until after he's fixed pancakes and read the front

section of the paper. At least until eleven-thirty. My clock said 8:26.

"Where are we going?"

"For me to know and you to find out. You've got thirty minutes to wash, dress, pack for a week and get to the street. I'm going to get the car. We'll grab breakfast on the way."

I groaned out of bed. Dad was already at the door. "A week? I can't go away for a week. I told you, we've got our first gig at Sissy Klein's party next Saturday. We've got to practice. Max and Ben are counting on me."

"We'll discuss it on the way."

Translation: *No discussion. You're going.* I thought about going over to Max's house. If Dad came to get me I'd refuse to leave. Then the picture of Dad getting teary-eyed at me popped up in my head. I couldn't do it. It was a pretty asinine idea anyway.

The jangling sleigh bells told me he'd left the apartment. I punched Max's number on my cell. I'd almost called him lots of times the night before, but what was I going to tell him? "Hey Max, you remember that girl I told you about? You won't believe what she and Mom were doing." Maybe I could have just told him how beautiful An-ling looked naked, but that was mine to keep. Now Max was going to kill me for waking him up, but I had to tell him that even if Mom and Dad dragged me to Alaska, nothing was going to stop me from playing at Sissy Klein's birthday party.

"The party you are trying to reach is not available. Please try your call again later."

Fuck James Earl Jones. Fuck Max.

Washing, I decided, meant brushing my teeth, that's it. Dad had already gotten my duffel bag out of the hallway closet. I couldn't find any clean jockeys. Where was Mom? Their bedroom door was closed. I opened it, ready to see her fully dressed, leaning over a suitcase on the bed, holding up one shirt then another, never making up her mind. She always ended up taking too much. Maybe we could both gang up on Dad and stay put.

Only the top of Mom's head was showing above the sheet. Her breathing sounded hollow and far away, like all I was hearing was an echo. "Mom! I can't go away for a week. We're playing next Saturday and we've still got to get it together. Can't you talk to Dad?"

She sat up, dug her hands into her hair and stretched her eyes open. She had pillow marks on her cheek, two red welts, and her eyes were puffy.

"Why are you still in bed? Dad's picking us up in twenty minutes."

"You'll have fun just the two of you," she said after taking a minute, waking up, I guess. "Moms get in the way on trips like this."

Great! I'd have to fight Dad alone. "Do you know where we're going, at least?"

"He wants to surprise you."

I heard the buzzer from downstairs. One, two, three blasts. "Dad's waiting." She caught my shoulder and kissed my cheek. Her breath didn't smell good. "About yesterday with An-ling, I want you to know—"

I stopped her with a wave of my arm. "I don't have any clean jockeys."

"Look in the dryer. We'll talk when you get back."

"Sure. Bye."

"Have fun."

Halfway down the hall I heard, "Josh!" She was standing in the doorway of her bedroom, one pajama leg rolled up above her knee. It made her look crooked. "I love you, Sweetie."

It made me feel squishy and I didn't know if she expected me to go hug her or what. The buzzer blasted again.

"Bye, Mom." I ran to the kitchen and grabbed my jockeys from the dryer. On the table, propped up on Dad's dirty coffee mug, was an envelope with Mom's name on it in his handwriting. Probably our itinerary. He'd sealed it, which was a bummer. I splattered water in the mug and put it in the dishwasher, my goodbye present. The envelope ended up on top of the tea kettle, below the drawing of the ugly Chinese kitchen god An-ling had given Mom. That's where she'd see it for sure.

Mom, when she said she loved me, I should have told her I loved her too.

Dad drove up the coast, final destination—Maine. Any place facing water was a good food stop. Sometimes we went swimming. The water was freezing. He didn't talk much, just some stuff about the old days in places we were passing through. Who came over when from England, what battles they fought. I'm not big on history so I didn't really listen. Dad said it'll come later, when I'm older and get a sense of the importance of consequences, of how past events affect our lives, like I didn't know that already. Every once in a while I'd bring up the gig at Sissy Klein's.

"I know. I know," he'd say.

Dad started talking about his parents one night after he'd had a couple of beers. His father died in the Korean War.

"With Dad gone, right away I felt I had to be strong and good. I had to take care of my mother. Never mind that I was only five years old."

He still missed his dad. His mother died of a bad heart when he was in college.

"It hurt a lot. All loss is painful, but it teaches you things."

Sure, Dad, loss is great, I thought, but I could tell he was really into this, so I asked, "What things?"

"It steels you to tackle anything that comes your way. What seems terrible and frightening changes with time. Fades. You forget the hurt for long stretches. It's like a muscle you're not aware of. It might cramp up sometimes, then ease back."

I didn't buy the sometimes. My sister's death was a permanent cramp with him and Mom. That's what I thought he was talking about. I wished I could have a couple of beers too and find the guts to tell him he didn't have to hide Amy from me any more.

In a place called Sorrento, Dad paid a fisherman to take us out to check his traps. For almost two hours we watched Mike remove the lobsters from each trap, measure them and throw the little ones back in the water.

"You see, Josh? As long as you're young, you get a second chance," Dad said. "Consider yourself one lucky kid."

I wasn't sure what he was talking about this time. Maybe how he and Mom were getting old and maybe we shouldn't have gone off without her. Like maybe she'd think we didn't want her around anymore because of that one thing in the bathroom. All I could really think of was getting a second chance with An-ling naked, how I'd touch her all over and then maybe she'd let me in and we'd fuck for six days straight. And then I'd show up at Sissy's party and play better than Alvin Jones and Buddy Rich put together and maybe there'd be a music producer, a friend of Sissy's dad maybe, and he'd hear me and hand me a contract. That's the kind of dumb thinking I did on that boat.

Dad decided it was time I learned how to drive. We went out on the back roads when the sun was just coming up and the sky wasn't much lighter than the road I was trying to keep the car on. I couldn't see that far ahead, but Dad said that was good. It would keep me focused and at that hour the state police would care more about catching a cup of hot coffee than a thirteen-year-old kid driving. That was the best part of the trip. That and the lobsters, our visit to LL Bean and dreaming of sex.

Every night Dad reminded me to call Mom. She was never home. I didn't leave messages. I wasn't going to play messenger boy for them. She had my cell number. And why wasn't Dad picking up the phone to call her? I did catch him once, in the middle of the night, sliding the cell phone out from my backpack and slipping out of our motel room. He wasn't gone more than a minute or two. They didn't need to say a lot, just "Hello, we're fine. How about you? That's good. Bye now."

I called Max. It was hard to practice without me, he said. "You give us the beat, you know. That's the drummer's job. To keep us in check."

Maybe I should have given my parents the beat.

Friday morning, we were in Kittery, just across the state line from New Hampshire, having breakfast by the water-side on our way back home. I was going to get to play at Sissy's party; the water couldn't have been bluer and the waitress had just plunked my second order of blueberry pancakes right down on the table. Life was rocking.

Dad asked, "How did you like the trip?"

"Super, Dad. Thanks."

"You're not mad I took you away from your drum kit?"

I shrugged. "I've got the beat down cold."

"Not too boring with just your old Dad?"

"You're not that old!" He looked so needy I was embar-rassed. "It's not boring. I told you, it's been great. Thank you, thank you, thank you." I stuffed my mouth with pancake, hoping Dad would change the subject.

"How would you feel if it was just the two of us for a bit?"

I stopped chewing. "What do you mean?"

"I'm just asking."

He tried to smile, but didn't make it. I tried swallow-ing—the pancake had turned into sand. This trip out of nowhere. Mom telling me she loved me out of nowhere, not coming along. Her not being home and not calling. It all came together. "You and Mom are splitting up, right?"

"No, Josh."

"I don't believe you!" I jumped up, hitting my hip against the table, tipping it. My plate vaulted into the water, pancakes flying. "Great! Just great!"

"It's all right, Josh. It's not your fault."

What wasn't my fault? I stared at the floating pancakes, not ready to look at Dad. The seagulls' wings made a dry, crackling sound as they swooped down. I got a perverse satisfaction out of watching them tear at the pancakes, hearing them scream at each other, slapping their wings around.

"What happened, Dad?" I asked in the car.

"You're jumping to conclusions."

"Then why did you bring it up?"

"Your mother might need to go away for a while and it's better to see it coming and be prepared. And then if she doesn't, we'll be all the happier."

"Why does she need to go away? Does this have something to do with An-ling?"

"I'm sorry. Forget about it. I was just testing the water."

"Dad, talk to me."

He patted my knee, again tried a smile. This one almost made it. "It'll be okay. Don't worry. You want to drive?"

It was way past cops-chasing-hot-cups-of-coffee time. "I'll get arrested."

"A fine at the most, which I'll pay."

"Thanks, but no thanks."

At lunch, over hot dogs, I tried again. "Why does Mom want to leave?"

"Maybe she just needs a break from us."

"Is that why we left without her?"

"In part."

"So then it's fine. She's had her break."

"She might want more time. Could you handle that?"

"How about you?"

"I'll make do if you will."

I'd just been given the job of holding him up in case Mom decided to leave us. "Sure," I said, like it was no big deal one way or the other. Was it Mom, or did he want out? I didn't know, but on the drive back I thought about how I hadn't really missed Mom during the trip, not the kind of missing that hurts. But then I was sure she'd be there when I got back.

One thing I've learned about my dad is that he believes in keeping the bad hidden. Not a word said. Even if it makes things worse. I guess that's where I get it from.

If Mom gets convicted, what'll I do? Let it be?

Subj: Fairytales and fantasies
Date: 04-10-05 23:31.53 EST
From: Chinesecanary@BetterLateThanNever.com
To: EPerotti@aol.com

What is significant in traditional Chinese painting is what is left unpainted. I know I should leave a lot untold. What little shine I have left in your eyes would stay, but here goes:

My legal name is Jean.

Jean Owens. Forget it. That name is history.

They said they didn't know my Chinese name. They lied. I found it written on the birth papers Hannah kept in her closet. It really is An-ling. I like to think it's the name my mother gave me, not the orphanage.

My lie #308

I didn't quit Dr. Feldman. He fired me because I told a client that no matter what she did to her wrinkles, she'd still be an old woman. I didn't want you to think I was asking for a handout.

A-l

Emma

A futon, on which I was sitting, two bed sheets tied into fat balls stuffed with clothes, art supplies and twenty-two canvases—the sum of An-ling's possessions—crowded one corner of the studio. An-ling untied one sheet and fished around in the jumble of socks, undies, T-shirts, shoes. I was only too glad to rest against the wall and watch. A rain-heavy sky filled the windows, giving off an ashen light that, combined with the August heat, lulled the anger I'd kept inside me for three days, since Tom and Josh left. "We need to breathe some clean air," Tom had written in his note. I started to call Josh's cell many times—Tom doesn't own one—then stopped, not sure my call would be welcome. When the phone rang, I let the machine pick up, afraid I would lash out at Tom for leaving me, at Josh for going with him. There were no messages.

"We'll have to get you some furniture," I said.

"I'll go to the Salvation Army. You've done enough. Ah, here they are." She held up two coiled strips of red satin against her chest.

I wanted to bring up Amy, tell her that Josh knew nothing, ask her not to break our silence, but her face was as bright as the cloth. She was happy.

"What are those?" I asked. Another moment would come. "*Duilan*. I'm hanging them on each side of the front door to keep my new home safe." She let the two strips unfurl along the length of her thighs. To my surprise, the words, handwritten in gold ink, were in English:

A house full of light is good fortune.

A good friend is a gift from heaven.

I felt a swaying inside me, as though some cheerful tune had been turned on.

"Keep your new home safe from what?"

"Masons and carpenters have great knowledge of bad spells. They leave things to hurt you. A sword with a silk string tied around it will bring anger in the house. A shoe, a thread dipped in ink, blood, these are all bad things they may have left behind. I'm not sure I believe it, but there are so many bad people in the world, it could be true." She let the satin strips flutter down to the futon.

"There is also this." An-ling fingered through the canvases stacked on the facing wall and lifted the largest one. "Portrait of my new boyfriend." She turned it around with a sly smile. A warrior in battle dress, with menacing black eyebrows, pop-out eyes and a scowl straight out of a cartoon, swung a sword above his head, one foot raised, ready to stomp on his enemies while bats flew over his head. The colors were loud, garish.

I laughed. "You've got terrible taste in men."

"Emma! You're supposed to be scared. He's Zhong Kui, the demon slayer. Our St. George. He will protect me from intruders."

"You should take him on the subway with you."

"You're making fun of me."

"I'm teasing, trying to get you not to be so fearful. If you keep your eyes open and your door locked, no one will harm you."

"I've been taught to be afraid of such good fortune. I'm not really superstitious, but the old traditions are the way of my ancestors, the way of the China that Mao tried to kill. I want to honor that."

I stood up and gave her a quick kiss on the side of her head. "Good for you. I'll get the hammer and a nail. Where do you want to hang St. George?"

"I think above my futon. Just in case my ancestors were on to something."

For the rest of the day we hung blinds, nailed An-ling's paintings on the walls, and wandered the new neighborhood to shop for food and household goods. Over lunch and dinner, eaten squatting on the floor, An-ling chattered about her fellow students at the Art Students League and about her new job in the admissions office. How she was going to work to be the best painter in the city. As the day passed, I absorbed her eagerness, her hope. I said nothing about Amy or Josh.

The windows turned dark. A halo of dull light rose above the Manhattan skyline. "Stay with me," An-ling said. There was no reason to go. No one was home. She insisted

I take her futon while she curled up on the mountain of her tangled clothes. For the first time in months I slept through the night.

The next morning, while I was out getting breakfast, she ordered a mattress. "For when the guys go away again," she said when it was delivered. She wouldn't let me pay for it.

Two days later, as I was getting ready to go home, she stuffed a bag full of M&Ms into my handbag.

"For Tom and Josh."

Her sweetness gave me courage. "You know about Amy."

She looked taken aback for a moment, then walked across the room to sit on her futon. "I wanted to say I'm sorry you suffered so much, but Amy is your secret."

I sat down next to her, surprised I felt only relief. No shame. "How did you find out?"

"A teacher at the League recognized you when you came to visit that one time. She grew up in Mapleton."

"Why did you tell Tom and not me?"

"It doesn't matter if he gets angry."

I took hold of her hand. "We never told Josh. It would have been a terrible burden for him. Even worse now."

"You can trust me."

"I do. I hope you still trust me."

"Don't worry, Lady Teacher. I don't blame you."

I studied her face but could not read it. I needed to believe her too much. "Thank you. You may be the only one who doesn't."

Back at the apartment I waited for Tom and Josh to come home and wondered if, after Amy's death, trust had ever resided in our home.

ELEVEN

TOD CURTIS, A tall, hefty painter and sculptor in his late forties, rents the loft directly above An-ling Huang's. He is wearing chinos, running shoes, and a black T-shirt.

"Where were you on March thirtieth of last year?" Guzman asks.

"In my loft, preparing for a show that is now up at the Sogni Gallery in Chelsea. I didn't leave it all day. Or night for that matter."

"Did you, in the course of that day, hear anything out of the ordinary?"

"Yes. In the morning, around eleven o'clock, the defendant and the girl, An-ling, started fighting. They were very loud. I had to turn up Mahler—the *Fifth Symphony*—to drown them out. I always listen to music when I'm painting. It unleashes the imagination."

"Can you describe the fight."

"Not really. I heard 'What you did was vile, disgusting!' That's it, I'm afraid."

"Were you able to recognize the voice?"

"Her." He points. "The defendant."

"Emma Perotti?"

"No doubt about it."

Emma

"Have you made up your mind?" Tom lowered his dinner plate into the sink. I was still at the table, eating grapes. Josh was in his room, studying. School had started. In the ten days since they'd come back from Maine, we had gone about our family business—eating together, asking routine questions, giving each other goodnight pecks—in slow motion and with great deliberation. The air around us had turned to sludge.

"Made up my mind about what?" I dropped a grape in my mouth.

"Are you still seeing An-ling?"

The fruit was tart, filled with seeds. "Yes." I spit the seeds out. I'd seen her only once after my two-day stay with her. A quick lunch between her classes. "The M&Ms Josh gobbled up were a present from her for the two of you. She says sweetness breaks curses."

"I asked you not to see her."

"She found out about Amy from an art teacher who used to live in Mapleton." His face registered disbelief. "Our guilty secret is safe, Tom. She won't tell."

Tom splashed water in the sink, turned off the faucet. "That girl's no good."

"You have no idea what's she's like. You've never given her a chance. I'm going to help her for as long as I can," I told Tom's back as he left the kitchen.

That night Tom moved into the study. Over the next few weeks Josh spent a great deal of time with Max. Whenever he was home and I asked to talk to him, he shielded himself with a test to study for, a paper to write, a song to rehearse, an urgent call to make to Max. Scared that he too would ask me to give An-ling up, I didn't insist.

I felt marooned.

When not teaching, while Josh was still at school, I would take the train to DUMBO. I brought flowers to An-ling's loft, cleaned up, ran the washing machine and dryer my colleague had left behind. I filled the refrigerator with food, scoured the junk shops in the area for furniture that An-ling might like and that she could afford. I sat on a stool by the window overlooking the bridge and the slice of the East River and fed on the brilliance of September in that loft. Being there suffused me with warmth.

When An-ling found me in her home, she would clap her hands. "A hundred happiness frogs leap in my heart. Please stay. It's lonely at night."

By late afternoon I'd be back in Manhattan as Tom's wife, Josh's mother.

"Do you know what you're doing to Josh?" Tom hurled at me one night from the doorway of the bathroom while my mouth was full of toothpaste. "He's sick to his stomach. His mother panting after some girl like a dog in heat. A girl who's only after what she can get out of you. God damn it, Emma, Josh is your son! He should come first."

I spit out the toothpaste. "An-ling is not my lover!"

He steeped into the bathroom and closed the door. "You love her like a daughter, right?"

"Yes, that's exactly right."

"How can you say that to me?" His voice was low, raw with emotion. "That girl is nothing like Amy. No one can replace Amy. She's dead. You killed her, remember? You can't get her back!"

I let the cruelty of Tom's words steep until I started to believe he had no love left for me. In the years since Amy, anger had whittled away what good feelings he'd had. For fifteen years we had walked through our married life on opposite sides of a chasm. I knew it all along, I told myself. How could I not? And yet it was only now, leaning over the sink with toothpaste dribbling out of my mouth, that I realized how insurmountable the distance between us had become.

His face moved into the mirror. "Leave. Move in with her. Play mommy or lover around the clock. Get it out of your system. We'll do fine without you."

He wanted me to go. Just him and Josh, without the killer mom, the way he must have always wanted it. An-ling was his excuse. Our excuse.

On cross-examination, Fishkin asks, "Mr. Curtis, in the five months you and Emma Perotti lived in the same building, how many times did you speak to her?"

"Hard to say. Eight, ten times maybe."

"Where did you speak to her?"

"In the elevator."

"How many minutes would you say is the ride to the fifth floor where she lived?"

Curtis looks annoyed. "I never timed it, but I'd say two, three minutes. It's a real old elevator."

"What did the two of you talk about during that brief period?"

"Hell, I don't remember. Nothing earth-shattering, I guess." Curtis raises an arm, exposing a streak of iridescent orange paint. "Wait a minute. One time she asked me to come look at the girl's work. She wanted me to help her find a gallery. I told her I had my hands full promoting my own work."

"How did she react to your refusal?"

"She was always a cool lady. You know, the type that keeps her baggage under lock and key."

"Having exchanged two- or three-minute conversations with Emma Perotti eight or ten times over five months, you say that you recognized her shouting voice one floor below, while listening to Mahler and concentrating on your painting?"

"Yup. She's got a furry voice. Sexy."

"Even when she shouts?"

Curtis's eyes dart to Guzman. There's a moment's hesitation before he answers. "Yes, even then."

Josh

It was about a month after the trip to Maine, a month when it felt like the iceberg that sank the Titanic had surfaced in our apartment. I was in bed, almost asleep. I heard a click, felt heat on my face. Then I heard Mom's "furry" voice. "I want to talk to you about An-ling."

I unscrunched an eye. She was standing over my bed. I poked my nose out from under the bedcovers and opened the other eye. The lamp lit her from the waist on down. "Your father thinks you're upset." Her knees stuck out of her bathrobe. They looked like old wrinkled faces. "Are you upset?" Her face stayed in the dark.

"What, Mom?"

"Are you upset that I see her a lot? That I'm helping her?"

I shook my head. Shaking your head is like a twitch, something that can happen even if you don't want it to. It's not like downright lying, because the truth is, that while I wasn't what I'd call upset, I did wonder what the hell was going on.

"I've tried to tell you we're just friends. Our relationship is a perfectly normal one."

"You've got to work it out with Dad. It's got nothing to do with me."

"He wants me to give her up or leave and if I give her up—" she sucked in her breath, a quick sizzle of a sound.

"What?"

"It would be cruel. An-ling has no one in this country except us."

I sat up. This was it, what Dad was preparing me for in Maine. "You do what you want to do, Mom. Don't ask me to make up your mind for you."

She grabbed hold of my neck, kissed the top of my head. I could smell the perfume she uses—One by Calvin Klein.

Dad and I give her a bottle every Christmas. Remembering that made my stomach feel funny, caved in.

"You love your father very much."

"Sure."

"You're best buddies."

"Yeah." I didn't know where she was going with that. I mean, she knew this stuff already. I don't know. Maybe she was jealous. She wanted me to tell her how much I loved her. I didn't because, well, I just didn't. Which didn't mean I didn't love her.

"Go stay with her for a while, if you want," I said. "It's okay. We'll be okay." That was what she wanted to hear, I thought. Now I'm not so sure.

Tom

Friday of Columbus Day weekend I had one of my cravings for ice cream in the middle of the night. I opened the freezer and was confronted with a wall of food. Every inch of space was crammed with stews from our favorite takeout place on Broadway, hamburger meat, chicken breasts, spinach, corn, pizzas, supermarket lasagna, Mars bars for Josh.

I shook Emma awake. "What the hell is all that food doing in our freezer?"

She turned over, mumbled. "It's just food."

I shook her shoulder. "There's enough to get us through the entire winter."

She sat up, pulled the blanket up under her chin. All she let me see was her face streaked with pillow marks. "I'm going away for a few days. I've discussed it with Josh and he's okay with it. It'll do us both good. Please don't make it a big deal, Tom. It's something you want too. As you pointed out, you and Josh will do fine without me. The two of you are a kingdom unto yourselves."

"I want no such thing!"

"I'm going."

She stared at me, waiting for me to fight her. Instead, my anger walked me out of the bedroom, back to the kitchen. I sat in the cold light of the open freezer and dug into a pint of strawberry ice cream. Anger got mixed with humiliation, with love, with grief. The new grief touched upon the old one of Amy being gone, went further back in time to the stunned silent grief of when my mother died.

For the duration of that pint, I cried tears I didn't know I had in me. Then I threw that self-pity in the garbage with the ice cream carton and went back to the bedroom. She was waiting for me.

"How long is a few days?"

"That depends on you."

"No, it doesn't." Again I walked. Josh and I were indeed a kingdom unto ourselves.

My wife left on Columbus Day. I wonder if she was aware of the irony of that date.

I didn't ask Emma to leave our home, I told myself in the days that followed. Nothing would drive me to separate my son from his mother. By giving her a choice I was trying to jolt her mind, to clear it. I was presuming she was still a mature, responsible individual. I was assuming she could

assess the consequences of her behavior, the damage to Josh, to our marriage. When I gave Emma a choice I had no doubts that she would stay. Her family or that girl—it was an absurd juxtaposition. It was no choice at all.

TWELVE

Josh

THE SUNDAY AFTER
for brunch on Avenue B—Alphabet City
Dad said was full of muggers and drug
Mom's cheeks. "How'd you know about t
here? Why not in Brooklyn near An-ling's p
in Morningside Heights, near me?

She pecked back. "I don't remember," she sai
voice, like her throat was bothering her, like she di
me to know An-ling was showing her a whole new

We sat by the window in a corner of a long, narrow
with polished metal walls and furniture that made me
I owned sunglasses. Outside, couples walked past, holdi
hands or pushing strollers. No dealers I could spot.

171

"How are you?" she asked, after she ordered eggs benedict. I went for French toast.

"Fine." The chair I was sitting in dug into my back. I put my down jacket back on. "Lots of work at school, but I can handle it. Practice with Max and Ben. You know, the usual."

"Dad?"

"He's okay. He's working big time."

Her eyes stayed glued on my face. Did she forget what I looked like?

"Stop it, Mom."

She gave a tinkle of a laugh. "You're becoming so good-looking."

"In a week?"

The food came, which gave her an excuse not to answer that. The French toast was thick, the way I like it. "We got a cleaning lady on Friday"—my mouth was half full—"from Mrs. Ricklin. Soledad. She's from Guatemala. She's going to come twice a week."

Mom's fork stopped halfway to her mouth. The egg dripped on the edge of the table, then slid down and landed on her lap.

"Just until you come back."

She put her fork down. "Do you like her?"

What did she want me to say? That I hated Soledad, that she could never replace Mom? I opted for the truth. "She's really nice and I thank her a lot. You always tell me not to exploit people. 'Gracias, Señora Soledad. Gracias para Usted trabajo.' It makes her laugh. That's good, isn't it?"

She wiped at her lap with a napkin. "She'll help with your Spanish." Her face stayed as cold as those metal walls.

After that, not much got said that meant anything in the situation. Mom drank three cups of coffee while I finished my toast. The rest of her food stayed on her plate. I should never have told her about Soledad. It made it look like Dad didn't want her back. "Mrs. Ricklin said Soledad needed to make a few extra dollars to help pay for her son's college,"—not true but why not?—"so Dad thought why not help her and help us? I mean when you come back she'll stay if you want her to. You know, it was just . . . why not?"

Mom paid the check, put on her jacket, flashed me a half smile. "I'm glad someone is helping." She walked me to the subway station on 14th Street. "Thanks for coming." I got a hug. "Next Sunday?"

So what happened to "a few days"? I wanted to ask, but didn't. "Sure. Next Sunday."

That was the start of our routine. She called a couple of times a week, always on my cell, then on Sunday, brunch. Greenwich Village became our meeting place. "The halfway point," she called it, which could mean two things: the halfway point between Brooklyn and the Upper West Side or the point where two opposing sides meet for truce talks.

During those brunches I wanted to ask Mom, "Is it great to be with An-ling? Is that why you're not coming home? Is she naked a lot?" I wanted to tell her how jealous I was, how I thought about An-ling every night. Instead I told her about the school principal sliding on a pretzel bag in the hallway and breaking his ankle, about Soledad ironing my T-shirts even after I'd asked her not to and earning me more dork points with the girls, about how Max had hired the trio for his own birthday party. How I was planning a series of portraits of my fish for photography class: The Fishtank Family Gallery.

She didn't offer much from her end. No touchy-feely conversations between us like: *I miss you. Do you miss me? Will you ever forgive me? I really do love you. I love you, but I also love her. I want you both; it's killing me. Tell me you understand.*

I would have said, "Sure Mom, I understand, but what about Dad? What about Dad's favorite mantra: self-absorption is the scourge of modern-day youth? What's your take on that, Mom? What's the age limit on youth?"

"How is your mother?" Dad always asked when I got home, his face looking like he was trying to loosen a really tight screw. There was always some written thing on his lap, like he was searching for a formula, some economic law that was going to balance things out again.

"She's good." It had to be good. Why else stay away?

A few days before Thanksgiving the phone rang while Dad and I were in the kitchen digging through Soledad's tamales. Dad picked up, listened. By the sharp set of his jaw I knew it was Mom. I started to leave, but Dad tapped my shoulder. He cradled the phone against his chest.

"Your mother wants to come home to cook Thanksgiving dinner for us. It doesn't mean she's going to stay."

"Did she say that?"

Dad's eyes turned soapy like he'd suddenly gone blind. It was up to me.

"Sure. Sounds good." Awful—a couple of hours chomping on food together, then the bell rings, family session's over and it's just me and Dad again. Hell on Dad.

"Fine," Dad said to the phone in his no-nonsense-tolerated voice. "What do you want me to buy?" He reached for the pad. I handed him a pencil. Then a long pause during which he turned his back to me, phone clamped tight against his ear.

"No," he said and hung up. He sat down, picked up his fork. "We'll go out for Thanksgiving. Some inn out of the city. The fresh air will do us good."

Mom wasn't invited, that much I knew, and I also knew not to ask what had happened. The unspoken is the M.O. around here and I've gotten to be an ace at reading the silence. Most of the time. The blade in Dad's voice only came out if An-ling was mentioned. Mom must have asked if she could bring her along.

For my fourteenth birthday, Mom suggested lunch—the three of us. Dad said he couldn't make it, which was just fine. The two of them faking nice on my birthday, no thanks.

December 6, a Saturday with lots of sun. Mom and I celebrated by eating great pasta at Lupa in the Village. She gave me a gift certificate for Drummer's World. I nearly choked on a fettuccini when I saw how much it was for. After lunch we sat on a park bench in Washington Square Park. "Dad's taking me to Pittsburgh for Christmas," I said. In the dog run, a black-and-white terrier was trying to mount a panting Lab.

She closed her eyes, pressed her lips together. I felt a little swish of satisfaction that I'd surprised her, that she didn't like the news. "We're visiting one of his college buddies, Sam somebody and his family. You know him?" The Lab sat down and put an end to the love affair.

"I was going to take you to a restaurant where you could order all the lobster Fra Diavolo you wanted."

My favorite food. "With An-ling, too?"

"No, just you and me. And Dad if he wanted to. I'll miss you."

I kicked a stone real hard and almost hit a passerby. "No, you won't!" I limped down the walkway, my toe killing me. I heard her running.

She tugged at my arm. "Josh, come back. Sit down, please."

"I got a headache." I kept on walking.

"All right, it's my fault," she yelled. "All of it. I'm a terrible wife, a terrible mother and I'm sorry. I'm sorry!" She didn't follow me, which was fine with me. When I ducked into a sidestreet I called Max, but he wasn't at his place and there was no way I was going home early to face Dad.

I ended up walking real slow on Sixth Avenue, then hitting Broadway at 34th Street and taking it all the way home, about a hundred blocks in all, my sore toe screaming at me the whole time, which somehow made me feel heroic. Along the way I made up my mind that if Mom wanted to see me, she'd have to come home.

The following Sunday she was smiling and I was eating Lobster Fra Diavolo and telling her about how *The Tale of Two Cities* was a boring book.

"Why doesn't An-ling ever come with you?" I asked.

"This is our special time, just you and me."

"I'll go back with you. I want to see where you live."

"Maybe when you come back from Pittsburgh."

In bed at night I imagined the place she'd gone to: a humongous white cave full of light, like the lofts I'd seen in the movies. They would never lose sight of each other: Mom reading or correcting papers at one end of the place, An-ling painting at the other end. They could wave to each other, shout to be heard. At night they could curl up in bed and listen to each other breathing and never be scared of being alone. I'd see An-ling getting up in the middle of the night: She's naked and the light from the street shines on her body as she walks toward me across the floor. She continues to walk, getting bigger and bigger until I came in my hand.

The Sunday before Christmas it was real cold and Mom took me to a crowded Italian coffee shop on MacDougal Street after our brunch. She started telling me how coming down to Greenwich Village was the *it* thing to do when she was at Queens College, how she and her girlfriends would sit in this same coffee shop and order espresso after espresso until their hands trembled from the caffeine.

"We were trying so hard to be sophisticated Manhattanites." She spread out her hands and started pinching her fingers. The windows were all steamed up from the heat in the place, but she kept her gloves on, which meant we weren't going to stay for long. A quick bite, a coffee for her and then we'd head for my subway on Christopher Street and she'd go back to Sixth Avenue to get the F train— I'd studied the route on a subway map—back to An-ling.

"Now I can only drink decaf," she said.

"What about your friends?"

"I lost touch when I got married."

"Let's go to the loft, Mom."

She shook her head, the smile stuck on her face like a bubble-gum balloon that had popped before she could get it back into her mouth. "Everything is still a mess. After Christmas."

Inside me, it felt like the wind had just died. I watched her pinch her thumb, forefinger, middle finger, down the line of one hand, down the other hand and back again.

She was never going to take me.

"Did I tell you I'll be coming in on Saturday mornings?" The smile got unstuck and swooped across her lips. "I start teaching extra classes after the Christmas holidays. Saturdays, nine to one. If you'd like, we could meet for lunch both days."

I told her Saturday was my day with Dad, which was more or less true.

The day she'd left us, Columbus Day, she'd come downstairs to the basement and sat on a trunk. I kept playing because what could I say? *Bye Mom, have a good time. Don't forget to send a postcard.*

"Call me whenever you want. If you want to talk or see me. Really, Josh, I mean it. Call me about anything." She slipped a note in my shirt pocket. "That's An-ling's phone number, but my cell's best. She doesn't have an answering machine."

"You call," I said. "On my cell."

She stood there while I played. We'd already gotten the "I love yous" out of the way earlier. I didn't know what she wanted now. Her eyes were red and mushy, but why was beyond me, since she was doing what I thought she wanted. I wasn't going to feel sorry for her. I wasn't going to beg her to stay.

I lost the beat at some point. "It's okay, Mom," I said. She didn't budge. "I'll call you."

I stood up. She stood up. I leaned over my drum kit and gave her a half-assed hug. She could have walked around the drums and wrapped her arms around me. I guess I could have done that too.

"It's just for a few days, Josh." She stood there for the longest time. I went back to my drums.

It never entered my head that maybe she was waiting for me to stop her.

Emma

I lay on a mattress on the floor, hidden by a screen made of four tall canvases An-ling had hinged together, on which she had painted branches laden with pomegranates as red and round as Christmas balls. Their bright color was meant to bring happiness. A rectangle of cold white light from the window rested on the lower part of my legs, reminding me of Nonna's crocheted blanket lying at the end of Josh's bed. Outside the window, a sky without limits, still a shock to my eyes after years of seeing walls outside my bedroom. In this loft I felt like a pioneer who had moved out west and discovered vast open spaces.

It was Christmas, a day to celebrate the birth of a son, a day that has always filled me with the dread of its unmet expectations. My eyes to the window, I let my mind reel back to the skylight above our bedroom in Westchester. Back then in the mornings I would listen, through the intercom, to Josh gurgling safely in his crib, and look up at that quadrant of sky and feel that, if I lifted my arm, I could touch it.

From behind the screen, An-ling's voice surprised me. "Half the morning is gone."

She had a talent for silent movement. After two months I was often still surprised to turn and find her at my elbow. I would look up from reading, expecting her to be sitting across from me, only to find her at the far end of the room. Josh and Tom announced their comings and goings from a distance, scuffling feet, jiggling keys, whistling, calling out for clean clothes, food, a missing sock. An-ling came and went on ghost feet and asked for nothing.

"Good morning, An-ling."

"Christmas is a lousy day!" She stayed behind the screen.

"Why is that?"

"Because you're sad. Invite Josh to visit. Call him now. Tell him I'll cook Millionaire's Chicken for him and next year he'll become fabulously rich." An arm sheathed in red curved around the end of the screen. My cell phone dropped between my feet.

I sat up. "Let me see you." She slipped around the screen on all fours and sat on her haunches in the rectangle of white light at the end of the mattress. Her hair was neatly gathered in a ponytail. Her knees peered at me from behind the careful fraying of her jeans. Over the jeans she wore her new red fleece shirt. Following Nonna's tradition of keeping Christmas Day free of material thoughts, we had opened our presents on Christmas Eve.

An-ling picked up the cell phone and held it out to me. "Call Josh."

"He's in Pittsburgh with Tom." I missed him terribly.

"Call him in Pittsburgh. He'll come when he's back."

I had called him the night before. Our conversation wasn't long. I think Tom was in the room. Josh was having a good time, but didn't enter into specifics. I managed to tell him I missed him, but when I tried to say, "I love you," shame stuffed my mouth. I ended up mumbling that I'd love to hear from him as soon as he got home. With my real family I had lost the ability to act on love. I needed lessons on demonstration techniques.

"Josh can't come here," I said. An-ling's warmth seeped into the blanket. "Tom threatens to file for divorce if I let Josh visit." He had written me a note at school after he had refused my attempt at a Thanksgiving reunion, the four of us. I didn't add that, in Tom's mind, she was the one Josh could have no part of.

"Tom is mean."

"He's angry. I've broken his rules."

"You're going to leave me soon, aren't you? All this is just for a little while, right? Until the clock strikes midnight or something like that."

"It doesn't mean I'll stop seeing you." Part of me wanted to extend this irresponsible interlude until the day An-ling slipped out the door, chasing a wish across the street, the river, the country. Another part wanted Josh. And Tom. The parts were at constant war. Tom and Josh were going to win, but I wasn't ready to leave yet. I was still too angry with Tom to walk back, too involved with An-ling. Dumbly, I still hoped I could keep all three in my life.

"It *is* a perfectly lousy day," An-ling said.

. . .

"How about throwing a New Year's Eve party?" I suggested while we finished the previous night's leftovers for lunch. We'd decided to treat this day like any other. I was preparing lesson plans and An-ling was lining up rows of the different-shaped bottles that it had taken us weeks to collect for a new series of paintings. "Invite all your friends. I'll help."

An-ling could be shy, aggressive, giddily happy, rude one moment, sweet enough to bring tears to my eyes another. Now she turned sullen. "I don't like parties."

I cleared the dishes. "OK. Then don't have one."

The next day, when I came back from grocery shopping, I found An-ling on the phone inviting someone over for New Year's Day. "Day is better," she said to me, as she dialed the next number. "I want to show off the light. They'll be purple with envy."

"Purple for rage, green for envy."

"They'll be a rainbow of colors! Eighteen, twenty people, is that too many?"

"Just right. I'll help you set up, then leave. I won't cramp your style."

"No way. You are honorable Lady Teacher." She turned on the radio and started to dance to Mendelssohn's *Scottish Symphony*. "This is the first party in my life."

I stopped giving parties in my home after Tom thought one of my students stole Josh's Discman. That was at least five years ago. I started dancing, too.

. . .

An-ling insisted on offering only homemade food. For two days we cleaned and cooked. I baked the cookies. For the rest of the menu I followed instructions. We chopped, churned, folded ground pork into small triangles, rolled chopped vegetables into spring roll wrappers, sealed dough with wet pinches. A few hours before her friends were due, she fried and steamed. I cleared An-ling's work table and set out paper cups, plates, and napkins.

Boots scraped up the stairs; then voices. There were doorbells downstairs, but no buzzer to let people in, and we had left the metal front door open with a note saying the hand-operated elevator was broken. It saved us from having to ferry people up and down. An-ling lived on the fifth floor but none of her friends had reached thirty, a fact I used to convince myself we weren't being selfish.

"Someone's coming," I called out as I slipped a tray of dumplings into the microwave. A first cluster of friends walked through the door. A blonde girl let out a shriek, revealing her tongue stud, and pointed to Zhong Kui, the demon slayer. That morning An-ling had moved him from his place above her futon. Too tall to fit above the front door, the canvas tilted ominously over whoever crossed the threshold. A guaranteed ice-breaker.

"He's the Chinese St. George. Don't worry, he's tied to a sturdy nail." I waved them in, introduced myself and pointed them to the food table. "Help yourself. Drinks are in the fridge."

Steve wore a ponytail of dreadlocks that fell below his shoulders and drank only tea. His painting of a black woman's hand cleaning a white refrigerator had just been selected for a group show in a Chelsea gallery.

Komiko, a tall stringbean of a Japanese Texan, wearing purple bangs and tight black, stuffed spring rolls in her mouth between deep drags of her cigarette. "I'm not into edgy or politics," she said.

"She paints meticulous flower arrangements that will never make it in the marketplace," whispered pink-cheeked Jeffrey, Caucasian, proudly gay, the Cassandra of the group. His artistic vision was the depiction of huge pale spider webs that were meant to point out how delusional our sense of freedom was. The others I forget.

I stayed out of the way, stepping out of my role as Honorable Lady Teacher, into one as Very Honorable Clean-Up Maid. I gathered beer bottles, half-eaten sandwiches and emptied ashtrays while An-ling wove through her guests as they ohhed and ahhed over the amount of space she had, the open view, the light. Her cheeks were flushed from the heat, the beer she was drinking and the joy of being young, talented, and surrounded by friends.

Hours later we sat on a sagging Salvation Army sofa. Her friends had gone. Most of the mess was in garbage bags. She chugged on a bottle of water. She was tired and had said little since everyone had left.

I got up and opened a window. An icy wind from the river swept in and cleared some of the smoke and my own stale body smell. The bottom edge of the sky was bleached by the lights of Manhattan. The rest of the night was black, unlimited. I took a deep breath. The air was cold enough

to crack lungs. Again my thoughts traveled back—a recur-
ring symptom of the holiday season and the wine—to
Nonna standing above me as my body shivered in the cold
water she poured over me every morning. How I hated her
for it, and yet, remembering, I was filled with good feeling.

"I had a good time," I said.

"Thanks for helping," An-ling said. "It was a wonderful
party, wasn't it?"

I closed the window and sat down next to her. "The best.
I loved seeing you have fun."

"Never in a million years could I imagine having such a
beautiful home, giving a party," An-ling said. "Before they
came I was scared. I thought this is too good. It can't last. I'll
drop the dish. The cloud is going to pass over the full moon.
A rooster is going to call in the moonlight. Then I heard you
in my head."

"What did I say?"

"Get over yourself."

"I don't think I would ever say that."

"Then you should. Anyway I chucked the Chinese
superstitions and had a great time. Thanks to you." She
pecked my cheek.

"You did most of the work." I leaned back against the
sofa. Nonna came into my head again. "On New Year's Day,
my Italian grandmother would stay in bed all day and refuse
all food to avoid indigestion. It was her way of making sure
nothing went wrong, because she believed that if the first
day of the year was a good one, the rest of the year was
going to be good too." I turned to An-ling. "According to
Nonna, we're going to have a great year."

She looked uncomfortable, as if she were sitting on a sharp-edged thought.

"What is it?"

"You're leaving soon."

"I have a son and a husband, An-ling. I've been gone from home too long."

"When?"

"I don't know yet." I needed to talk to Tom first.

She curled up against me. I lifted my arm and let her slide into it.

"I'll miss you so much." Her breath heaved, trembled. I stroked her hair as she cried.

"I'm still here," I said.

Here's a fact: What I felt for An-ling had nothing to do with sex. Yes, I loved her body—the rough spots on her elbows that she would let me dampen with a sponge and rub with cream, the calm sea of her back on which the blue junk sailed, the half-shells of skin hooding her eyes, the powerful silent sway of her walk. Most of all, the triangle of her face, happy one time, sad another, a moody flower of a face, opening and closing at the least touch.

I never violated her body. Never had the desire. I held her when she needed me to. I kissed her cheeks, stroked her hair. In my bathroom she gave me a child's kiss on the lips. I gave back a mother's kiss.

Subj: Fairytales and fantasies
Date: 04-11-05 00:31.53 EST
From: Chinesecanary@BetterLateThan Never.com
To: EPerotti@aol.com

Explanations for Bad Behavior

"Careless, dumb girl." The round-eyed woman used to call me that a
lot and for a while I thought it might be the American pronunciation of
my true Chinese name. "Careless, dumb girl." I broke things. My
hands were too small to hold the dishes and the glasses in the sink.
The water made them slip. The shiver of splintering glass, the
whiplash of cracking china—terrifying sounds that sent me running to
the broom closet to hide. "Careless, dumb girl." The woman opened
the door and told me I had dripped all over the floor and my shoes had
left mud prints. She wrapped my hands over the stick of a mop. It was
an important lesson to learn, the need to clean up after yourself. It
would get me far in life, she promised. Besides, Chinese girls were
supposed to be obedient and clean and where did I come from if not
from China?

:-) :-(

An-ling

THIRTEEN

GUZMAN CALLS KOMIKO Tanuki to the stand. A Texan with Japanese parents, Tanuki was a fellow student of An-ling Huang's at the Art Students League. Today, in what she has said is a sign of mourning, she is dressed in a white tight-knit ankle-length dress and white sandals. She has sprayed her bangs with white paint.

"Miss Tanuki, was Miss Huang a good friend of yours?"

"Sure."

"Can you tell us what she was like?"

"She was shy. I'd push her to join us for a beer after class. Most of the time she didn't come. She did give a party at her new place on New Year's Day and invited a bunch of us, but she didn't really need other people."

Judge Sanders turns to the defense counsel with a barely hidden look of surprise. Fishkin stands. "No objection, Your Honor.

We welcome this witness's impressions."

Guzman glances at Fishkin, hesitates. Perhaps he is thinking that continuing this line of questioning may, in the end, come back to haunt him. Slowly he turns back to the witness. "What do you mean by Miss Huang not needing other people?"

"She was always running home to 'Lady Teacher.' That's what she called the defendant."

"Did Miss Huang explain her relationship to Mrs. Perotti?"

"She said she'd never been loved like that before."

"Did you have these conversations with Miss Huang in person?"

"We talked at school a lot. On our cells. Then, in March, I think, she bought a laptop from a student going back to Hong Kong and we started e-mailing, but before that sometimes she slipped notes inside my locker at the League."

"What did you do with those notes?"

"I kept every one. They were drawings torn out of her sketchbook that she'd scribble something on. I love her work." Tanuki's chin trembles. "Excuse me." She reaches in her pocket, takes out a tissue and blows her nose.

Guzman picks up two sheets of paper from his desk and hands them to the court clerk. "I offer People's Exhibit Twelve A and B in evidence."

After the exhibits have been labeled and given to the witness, Guzman asks. "Do you recognize those two drawings as being done by An-ling Huang?"

"I do."

"How do you know they are hers?"

"She signed them."

"Could you please read what Miss Huang wrote under the drawing in People's Exhibit Twelve A."

Tanuki reads silently, looks up and nods.

"Do you recall when you received this drawing?"

"Almost two years ago, late August sometime. This was her first one. We weren't sharing any classes yet."

"Please hold up the drawing so the jury can see it."

The drawing Tanuki holds out is a realistic depiction, in red ink, of a woman's naked torso. The woman's hands hold up two large breasts with exaggerated nipples.

"Miss Tanuki, please read what Miss Huang wrote underneath the drawing."

"Lady Teacher said my breasts are beautiful. By the way, you'll be happy. My hair's Asian again."

"Thank you. Would you now look at People's Exhibit Twelve B, please? Do you recall when you received that drawing?"

"January or February of last year."

"Please read what she wrote to the jury."

"I've hooked up with a kid. He's a virgin—WAS—which really turned me on."

"Show the drawing to the jury."

Tanuki turns the sheet of paper around to show a pencil drawing of a baby with an erect penis twice his size.

"Miss Tanuki, is there anyone in this courtroom, besides the defendant, who you have seen before?"

Tanuki points to the defendant's side of the courtroom. "That boy with the striped shirt."

"Where and when did you see the defendant's son, Joshua Howells?"

"Outside the League a couple of times in February when it rained the whole time. He was standing in the pouring rain without an umbrella, waiting for her. I asked An-ling if he was the kid that turned her on. She laughed and said it was none of my business."

"When did you see Miss Huang for the last time?"

"Two weeks before she died, after my mixed media class."

"Can you tell us about that meeting?"

"The usual. We smoked, talked about classes, about getting fat. I noticed she was wearing a St. Christopher medal on a chain around her neck. I'd never seen it before and I asked her where she got it. She told me the kid gave it to her."

Josh

That first time, the Saturday after New Year's, I stood at the corner and stared up at the windows, trying to figure out what floor they lived on, which windows were theirs. The curtains at home are striped so I looked for stripes, but I couldn't see any curtains. A couple of blinds were down. It was nine-fifteen on a Saturday morning. I guess people were still sleeping. What a genius! Here I'd spit-polished my "I'm looking for Mom" excuse for the whole hour and six minutes it took me to get to DUMBO and now I was going to wake up An-ling and really annoy her. On top of that, she was sure to take me for a thumb-sucking nerd who couldn't live without his mommy.

I left Mom's street and scoped the neighborhood. I played guessing games about which food shops they went to, decided on a coffee shop where Mom, if she hadn't changed, probably ordered her toasted English muffin without butter. It wasn't much of a neighborhood. Only a few stores with blocks of warehouses in between. Not a lot of people on the street. No artists hanging out, smoking some weed, doing their thing. No park, not one tree. The East River was behind buildings. I couldn't figure out why An-ling or Mom liked it. It was a dead area, nothing like where Dad and I lived. When I swiped my Metrocard at the subway turnstile I swore to myself I was never coming back.

The street Mom lived on sloped down to the river and the second time I went—the next Saturday—the temperature was about fourteen degrees and I kept walking down the slope, fighting the wind all the way, and then back up with the wind kicking my butt and the subway trains rattling over my head. I was working myself up to cross the street, run my eyes down the list of names for Huang/Perotti or Perotti/Huang and ring the doorbell. Or call An-ling up on my cell phone. I'd changed my excuse to "Sure, I know Mom's teaching, but I've got a friend—he's a neat guitar player—he lives ten minutes from here so I thought, if it's all right with you, I thought I'd see how things are going and let you show me the place. Unless you want me to come back when Mom's here?"

Too many words and I couldn't make up my mind on the approach. The cell phone seemed like the way to go. If she said no I could pretend I was still back home, miles from her, but using the cell made it a lot easier for her to say no. The cold had me wanting to pee and there was no way I was going up there and the first thing I'd be saying is, "Can I use your toilet?" By the time I got to the coffee shop eight blocks away and relieved myself I felt like such a doofus I went home.

On the third Saturday I crossed the street right away. I had six doorbells to choose from. Three just numbers, three with names: 1. M. Keller, 2., 3., 4. S. DePero, 5., 6. T. Curtis. Mom had to live in number 2, 3 or 5. After doing a Dad calculation, I rang DePero. He—I decided S. stood for Steve—lived between 3 and 5 which meant the possibility of his knowing Mom was double that of Keller who lived below 2 or Curtis, who lived above 5. If DePero knew Mom, maybe I could convince him to let me in. I wasn't sure what I was going to do after that.

When I got no answer from DePero I buzzed the others. Maybe artists are like musicians—stay up all night, sleep until the afternoon. I buzzed DePero again. For all I knew An-ling could have gone back to China and Mom was living alone or with another man: Keller, DePero, Curtis. An-ling could have just been an excuse. There were a hundred different ways it could go.

This time I kept my finger on the doorbell. That's when I noticed there was no speaker, which meant there wasn't a buzzer to let me in. That's when I used my cell.

She hugged me at the door downstairs, asked me why it took me so long to come over. She smelled like smoke, paint and something sweet, and she had this smile on her face, the kind that's easy to believe in because it was so wide that her cheeks bunched up like the tops of muffins. I wondered if she expected me to kiss her on the muffins or something, but her being so glad, so unsurprised, threw me. I shuffled my feet or did something equally inane. I skipped the kissing. I was sure I'd miss and poke her in the eye or bump into her nose and she'd widen those great hooded eyes and tell me I was a complete jerk. I took my baseball cap off.

"How do you like living with Mom?"

"Do you want to talk about her?" She ruffled the hair on top of my head where the cap must have flattened it out. It was weird because that's one of the things Mom does, that and straightening my jacket and lifting up my shirt collar.

"Is that why you're here? To talk about your Mom?" She sounded surprised.

I put my cap back on. "No. I want to see your place."

She folded the elevator gate to one side. "That's a good reason."

The elevator had grates for walls and was as big as my room. She offered to let me operate it, like I was a kid and needed a toy. I snapped my fingers. "Menswear on four and on the double." That made her laugh and up we went.

The place was small, nothing like I'd imagined. A ratty sofa, a couple of wooden chairs, a small round table next to the kitchen sink, one long table with An-ling's paint stuff on it. Lots of pictures on the wall with no frames. An-ling showed me where Mom slept, behind a screen, on a single mattress on the floor. An-ling slept in a futon on the other side of the room. I felt a little kick in my gut when I saw their sleeping arrangements. Part of me, the part that thinks like Dad, half expected a king-sized bed like Dad and Mom had at home.

She showed me this picture of a real ugly warrior—"The Roach Stomper," she called it—and then these red strips of paper with slushy sayings on them. The smell of the place was intense—smoke and her flower smell and paint—like there were a thousand An-lings in that loft. The smell of smoke always turned my stomach, but she was flicking a cigarette in a coffee can, looking me over as she talked and I felt like I'd walked onto the set of some arty foreign film. Everything was different, exotic. It was a place where you could do anything and no one would get upset or yell at you. I thought, that's why Mom stays here.

An-ling was wearing sweats big enough to fit Dad and I started to wonder what she looked like underneath, if she was wearing anything. "Thanks for the tour. I've got to go now."

"Not so soon." An-ling took the baseball cap off my head, held my chin in her hand. She said she wanted to paint me because I had good bones and a strong face while the models at her art school were either fat, old or blah. I went for the way she pressed her fingers down my face. Close up she looked warm and fuzzy, like she'd just got out of bed.

"I'm going to need you to sit for me, maybe three, four times. I'm going to sketch you now, but can you come back, Josh? Will you? I'm a perfectionist, which makes me real slow."

I stuffed my hands in my pockets, shrugged. "Okay with me." My heart slammed into my ribs.

"Don't tell Emma. Your portrait is going to be a surprise."

"Sure." The slower the better and I wasn't planning to tell Emma in the first place and I wasn't going to tell Tom either. They'd both have a fit. But I'd turned fourteen a month before and it was time I followed some of my own rules. I knew I was supposed to dislike this girl, hate her maybe, but I didn't. I thought it was okay, that nothing bad would come of my being there, wanting An-ling.

Subj: Fairytales and fantasies
Date: 04-11-05 02:19:01 EST
From: Chinesecanary@BetterLateThanNever.com
To: EPerotti@aol.com

You'd already left for your school to teach the new classes. I was look-ing at a milky sky and wishing for snow. Josh was standing under the streetlamp on the corner, by the hardware store. I thought of opening the window, waving to him, telling him to come up. I remembered the Irish story you read to me about the sick boy who stands out in the snow because his girlfriend is leaving and he loves her so much he doesn't want to live. Poor Josh. For a few minutes I felt like a thief for keeping you with me, but I knew you weren't going to stay with me much longer. He's your real child. He was going to get you back.

A-l

It is Fishkin's turn to cross examine the witness.

"Miss Tanuki, from what you have said of Miss Huang, it seems to me that, not only were you her best friend, you were her only friend at the Art Students League. Am I wrong?"

"I guess I was."

"To your knowledge, did she ever lie to you?"

Guzman half stands to object, then sits back down.

"Yes," Tanuki says.

"Please tell the jury about this lie."

"She said she was from Sun Valley. My folks have a place out there so I know Sun Valley. She thought Ketchum was ketchup and Warm Springs was in California. I don't know why she lied about that. She changed her stories a lot. One time she tells me Mrs. Perotti's husband wants to adopt her, then another time she tells me he's jealous and can't stand her. I don't know if that's lying or not."

"Did you confront her about her lie regarding Sun Valley?"

"Last winter we went for a beer with a bunch of students I'd just introduced her to and she gave them her 'I'm from Sun Valley, Idaho' story. I had one too many beers and told her she was full of shit."

"How did she react?"

"She cried a little, asked me to forgive her. Then she told me she was really from some small village in China, but she didn't want anyone to know because she was here illegally and they'd send her back. That was another lie. I don't know why she had to lie so much."

"How do you know she was lying this time?"

"Foreigners can't take classes at the League without showing them a visa of some kind."

"You told the jury that you saw An-ling for the last time two weeks before she died. Did you speak on the phone or receive an e-mail from her after that time?"

"No."

"Two weeks is a long time for friends of your age not to speak to each other. Had it happened before?"

Tanuki thinks for a moment. "No."

"You didn't try to reach her?"

"No. I was busy working on the end-of-year student show and I figured she was in one of her 'leave me alone' moods." Tanuki blows her nose again.

FOURTEEN

Emma

AN-LING BEGAN PICKING on me for silly things. Where had I hidden her black slacks, why did I move her paints, why couldn't I stop bugging her about her smoking? She wanted to know my schedule—when was I leaving, when was I coming back? When I asked her what was wrong, she laughed. "You're a worry-mama."

I tried to blame her testiness on the constant rain, on March madness, on her working too hard. I did not consider the effect my own growing unhappiness might have been having on her. I had lived with An-ling for five months, five months during which I was able to leave Amy's death behind me for hours at a time, during which I felt like a happy young mother again, a friend, thinking I was needed by her, even loved. Five long months during which I had also ached for my son, longed for my husband and waited. When I had walked out of my home "for a few days" I had not fully understood that it was Tom's intransigence, more than my desire to help and spend time with An-ling, that was sending me away. All this time I was waiting for him to call me home, to tell me that he understood my need to help An-ling, to reassure me that he loved me. Only then would I know that he'd finally forgiven me for Amy's death.

"It's time for me to leave," I told An-ling one morning, as she was slipping into her jeans.

She looked up, surprise on her face.

"I need to go back home."

"Not true." She glowered at me, one leg poised in mid-air like a horse ready to prance. "Don't go. Nothing's changed." Her leg slipped into the jeans.

"An-ling, I can't stay forever. I must go."

She buttoned up, took the raincoat and umbrella I held out to her.

"Remember to have fun," I called out, as she shut the door. We'd talk about it that night, over dinner, over the weekend. Maybe the rain would stop and we could talk during a long walk in Prospect Park. It was time to let An-ling fly on her own. Way past time to stop waiting for forgiveness. Time to go home to Josh, to Tom and what was left of our marriage. Time to face myself. Later I would call Tom and tell him I was coming home whether he wanted me to or not.

I looked down at the floor, streaked with dried mud. Now it was time to mop. I would start with An-ling's corner. I folded the screen against the wall, pushed the futon to one side.

Nothing had changed. Everything had changed. The proof lay on the floor.

She left it for me to find. That was the thought that kept spinning in my head. She left it for me to find. She left it for me to find. She left it for me to find. I felt myself hollow out, as if someone had stuck a hose down my throat and was vacuuming my insides.

A 12 × 16 inch painting of a young naked man from the neck down to his knees. He was sitting with his back to the screen behind which An-ling slept. One hand clasped a knee with spread fingers, the other was raised against his neck. A chain dangled between his fingers on the end of which hung a St. Christopher medal.

I knew what was written on the back of that medal: Celestina Fenoli, 11-5-1901. Nonna's maiden name and the date of her first communion. It was a gift from her mother, passed on to me by Nonna on my communion day, picked up by Josh from my jewelry box when he was five years old. He'd worn it ever since.

Even without the medal I would have recognized my son by the short fingers of his hands with their flat broad nails, by the slender slant of his neck, by the sickle-shaped scar above his knee. What was new to my eyes was his half-erect penis.

"The sinner's biggest desire is to be found out," the priest used to tell me at confession. "He knows that expiation will bring him peace."

"What is this?" I asked when An-ling came home. The painting was now hanging by itself on the back wall. I'd taken down all her other paintings, even the demon slayer and the duilan. There was nothing she could feast her eyes on except the headless portrait of Josh.

"My son is handsome. Why did you leave his head off?"

It was still raining hard and her hair streamed over her face in thin rivulets, hiding whatever expression she might have had. She threw her wet coat against the wall and sat on the floor to take off her shoes.

"Did you think I wouldn't recognize him?"

She walked to the stove in stockinged feet and lit the gas under the tea kettle, her jeans dripping water, leaving a thin dark trail.

"Answer me, please. I deserve that much consideration." She turned to face me, dangling the tea bag like Josh dangled his chain in the painting. Josh bent over a notebook or lying back on the sofa with his headphones on, listening to music, swinging the St. Christopher medal. It was his typical gesture of absorption, which I had witnessed countless times. How many times had she witnessed it?

"This is my son you've painted. Naked, aroused, and I want to know why."

The kettle started to whistle. She poured the water in a turquoise cup, dipped the tea bag in. "What exactly do you want to know? Why he had a hard-on? Why he was naked? Why I painted him?"

"An-ling. Please."

She walked up to me, pushed her hair back so I could see her face and kissed my cheek. "I'm sorry, but you're so suspicious. He didn't have a hard-on. I added that for fun. After painting trillions of naked men with drooping penises, it gets a little boring." She curled her legs underneath her on the sofa. "He came over one morning, looking for you. You should have seen the look of relief on his face when he saw that we sleep behind different screens. Is that what Tom and Josh think, that we're lovers? That the only reason you're with me is sex? That's pretty insulting."

"That's not what they think. Why didn't you tell me Josh came over? You shouldn't have let him in. I told you he must never come here. You shouldn't have let him in." My voice was shrill, petulant, but I couldn't help myself. I felt betrayed.

"He was downstairs. It was freezing cold. I let him in. Why are you so angry? Tom's never going to find out."

"Why didn't you tell me? Why did you keep it a secret?"

"He said you'd get mad if I told you. I believed him so I didn't. In exchange for the favor I asked him to sit for me. He's got good bones and private models cost fifteen bucks an hour."

"Did he have to be naked? He just turned fourteen."

"I can only see the bones if he's naked. He didn't care. And kids start to fuck at twelve, Lady Teacher. Time to get with the times."

Not Josh, I thought. He's too shy, too cautious. Not my boy. "How many times has he come over?"

"Twice. I work fast."

"The first time, what day was that?"

"About a month ago. Saturday morning."

"He knows I teach a class then."

"Maybe he forgot. You can't get mad at him."

"I don't want him back here and please get rid of that painting."

She unhooked the painting from the wall. "I'll paint over it. There's no reason for Josh to come back. He's seen the place. The painting is finished. He's never coming back."

I found myself not believing her.

The next day I told Inez Serrano, my boss, that I wouldn't be able to teach my classes that Saturday morning. She wanted a reason and my mind went blank.

"I'll put down sick leave," she said. I was so grateful to her that my eyes teared. I called Josh on his cell phone. He'd turned it off so I left a message. "Nothing important. Just wanted to know how you're doing. See you Sunday."

Saturday morning I dressed for school, made tea for An-ling, and left the mug at one end of her screen. She was still asleep or pretending to be. It had stopped raining and the radio announced that we would finally see the sun, a much-needed piece of good news as my plan involved standing behind one of the cars in the parking lot down the street to wait for Josh. When he came, if he came, I was going to wait half an hour, forty-five minutes maybe, and then climb the five flights of stairs to the loft, unlock the door, and see them together: laughing, sharing anecdotes like friends, like sister and brother. That's what I'd see.

Hiding in the parking lot, sneaking up on two people I loved dearly—it was like a scene from a tasteless movie.

"What the heck are you doing here?" Inez asked me when I walked into class half an hour late.

"Sickness come and gone," I told her.

Subj: Fairytales and fantasies
Date: 04-11-05 03:02:13 EST
From: Chinesecanary@BetterLateThanNever.com
To: EPerotti@aol.com

Josh came three times to our street. I watched him from the window. If Josh comes here, where we live, he'll take you back with him. That was my thought as I watched your son from my window.

Also I thought, what will he say to me, this boy? He'll cover me with insults, yell at me. "You're a thief!" And I'll bow my head to acknowledge the truth of his words. Or he'll say, "I miss her every day," and make me cry.

I didn't call to him.

"I want to see you," he said on the phone.

Josh called me. In your anger why did you forget that?

To a stranger you owe only a glass of water. Josh was your son and I welcomed him.

He brought no insults with him, just a sweet, embarrassed face. He wanted to see the place, he said, but he didn't look. His eyes stayed with me.

I invited him to come back. I wanted him here, sitting in front of me. Wanting me.

This time I would be the teacher. This feeling of counting, of being important in a good way, I wanted more. I've become a junkie.

You were the first to make me feel that An-ling Nai Huang deserved anything at all. Why did you love me so? I'm a throwaway girl. I warned you many times, but you didn't believe me. Now you see I was right and it's made you very angry.

Your throwaway girl :-(:-(:-(

Joey Thanapoulus owns a coffee shop at 200 Lowry Street. He's a wide, balding man in his fifties, with thick black eyebrows, a warm smile and sagging eyes. He is looking at a photograph of An-ling Huang.

"Did you ever see Miss Huang?" Guzman asks.

"I didn't know her name but when one of your cops showed me this picture, I recognized her right away. She was one of my regulars. A cup of tea and a bacon sandwich to go. Every day."

"Did she ever come in with the defendant?"

"Saturday morning, they'd be at my place. Ten o'clock, sometimes ten-thirty. The Chinese girl would have a bacon sandwich and the lady here an English muffin, no butter, and black decaf coffee." Thanapoulus taps his forehead. "Everybody's order's right here."

"Do you see anyone else in this courtroom who came to your coffee shop?"

Thanapoulus jerks up his chin. "The boy in the first row over there with the green, short-sleeved shirt."

All eyes turn to Josh Howells. Mr. Howells extends his arm toward his son, but the boy, red-faced, squirms out of reach.

"Can you remember when you first saw the defendant's son?"

"After Christmas the lady starts coming early on Saturday. Eight o'clock, for coffee to go. Maybe a couple of weeks later, half hour after she'd come and gone, the boy shows up."

"Did he come with Miss Huang?"

"One time. After that he comes in alone but orders her food. A bacon sandwich and tea to go. For him a Danish."

"Only on Saturdays?"

"Only on Saturday. Never on Sunday." He laughs at his own joke.

Fishkin forgoes cross-examining the witness.

Josh

Her mother tattooed a boat on her back, just above the hill of her butt. A Chinese boat, a junk with a quilted sail, about twice the size of my thumb.

"She was going to paint a seabird to protect me on the voyage, but I wanted a boat to cross the ocean."

I lay my cheek on the hill and blew on the boat. "I thought your mother died when you were twelve."

She turned over, her hip bumping my cheek. I landed on the flat of her stomach. I blew on her pubic hair, shifted my fingers through it. It was wet from me and her—sticky, bogged down with love like I was.

"In a dream my mother saw me swimming, my arms slicing the water, the waves falling open like two halves of a plum. She knew one day I would come to the States."

I spread myself on top of her, slipped my fingers between hers, stretched out both our arms, like the two bald eagles I'd seen on TV, interlocking claws and spinning through a dark blue sky. A bonding ritual, the narrator called it.

"These are the best of times and the worst of times," I said.

"That's from a book."

"That's how I feel. I can't say it any better. You're the greatest thing that's ever happened to me."

"What's the worst?"

"I don't like sneaking around. I don't like lying to my parents. To anyone. I think lies suck. I like stuff to be out in the open. Nothing's ever been open in my family and now I'm making it worse."

"I don't like lying to your Mom. I always feel like she's with me, her hand on my head, hot and heavy, tugging at me. She's great, but it gets to me sometimes." She brushed her hand over my chest. "I like you too much to give you up."

I kissed her, sucked at the smokey taste on her tongue.

"Why does Tom hate me?"

"He's mad, that's all. He doesn't hate you. You took Mom away. Do you think they'll get a divorce?"

"No, your dead sister will keep them together."

"What do you mean?"

"Guilt glue."

She straddled me, pushing down until I was deep inside her and I was suddenly in the eye of the hurricane. Everything around me was flying around, going crazy, but in the pit of my stomach I was in this incredible quiet spot, like a suspended beat between two notes. A place where nothing was ever going to be bad.

"Why me?" I asked, putting my pants back on.

"Because you're sweet. Because you won't hurt me."

I kissed her goodbye.

She held my jaw real tight between her hands. "You're not fucking me because you're trying to get back at your mother, are you?"

"No way. I love you." I was so full of love I could feel it on my skin, like sweat.

"Tell me again."

"I make love to you because you're the most wonderful, most beautiful girl I've ever met, the greatest thing that's ever happened to me."

"Tell me again."

"I love you."

"Then stay. The mountain is high and the emperor is far away."

"Not so far. Mom's class was over twenty minutes ago." I kissed her again, for a long time. I wanted to take the taste of her with me, on my tongue. It never lasted long enough. By the time I got to the subway stop I'd have to light a cigarette to try and get some of it back. "I miss you already."

"Promise you'll come back?"

"Always."

She reached into my shirt and unclasped my great grand-mother's chain with the St. Christopher medal.

"What are you doing?"

She slipped it in her pocket. "Now I know you'll come back."

Emma

Drummer Boy

Skin, stretched, longing.
Strike and a bud
Opens.
Petals widen, moist
With music made
By you.

A sheet of paper with An-ling's careful writing left carelessly on her paint table. Another sheet, a bed sheet from her futon, still wet with semen, left for me to wash. My ears roared. A train was coming over the bridge, heading straight at me.

I bit into the sheet, tore it with my hands. Strip after strip, like so many bandages that wouldn't stanch the wound.

"Why did you pick Josh?" I asked her when she came home. "Of all the boys you could have, why him?"

She stared back at me, lips in a pout of sullen defiance. I wanted to shake a response out of her. "Why, An-ling? I deserve an answer."

"Why not Josh?" she finally said.

"What have I done to you?"

She didn't bother to answer. What lay underneath my anger was pure pain. I felt kicked, spit upon. "Do you love him, is that why you did this?" I told myself I could forgive her if there was love.

"He's hungry for it," she yelled. "Hungry for love and for fucking. I give him the fucking. I don't have any love in me. You know what your son is doing? Do you get it? Fucking me, your son is telling you to fuck off. You deserve that for leaving him. He's your blood, your family. Leaving your own son, how is that not worse than my fucking him?"

I slapped her. "What you did is vile, disgusting!"

I lived in my office at school, slept in the hallway on the sofa. I joined the gym five blocks away so I could shower. Inez offered me her home. I refused. It was penance I was after, not comfort. The old Catholic habits die hard. At night I prayed, even as I didn't believe any Greater Power existed to hear me. I prayed out loud to listen to the drone of my voice, a lullaby to ease sleep. I prayed that my son would forgive me; I prayed to find forgiveness for myself. After my prayers I wrote a letter to my son:

"Dear Josh,

I killed your sister, ran her over. I loved her with my heart, my bones, my flesh, my breath. I loved her the way I had dreamed of being loved, the way any child should be loved.

When you came I was carrying a capsule of grief and guilt under my tongue as lethal as cyanide and I wanted to abort you. I thought I had no right to another child. I had already killed one baby; I could kill another. But as the days passed I began to feel you. You weren't much more than a cluster of cells, but I could picture you coiled inside me. I

*could picture you, a bloody mess between my legs, screaming
your head off. I could picture you suckling at my breast. I
could picture you growing into a fine young man.*

*I love you, Joshua Howells. I feel you with me, part of
me, the best part. I have always loved you, but I've been
afraid—knowing I didn't deserve you or the happiness loving you would bring. I was afraid of breaking my pact with
God, afraid retribution would be meted out and you would
suffer, and so, for all these foolish reasons that I know are
based only on superstition and ignorance, but that are so
imbedded in me that I could not shake them loose, I have
loved you in silence, behind a curtain of fear.*

*An-ling I loved because she reminded me of Amy, because
she was so openly in need of love, because I needed to love
openly. For these reasons I didn't want to give her up.*

*What you did with An-ling, behind my back, that came
out of anger. I understand that and I deserve your anger, but
now I'm asking you to forgive me. I want to come home.
Please give me another chance to be a good mother to you.*

*Love,
Mom*

Every night I wrote the same letter. Only a few words
varied. I tried to explain myself, even though part of me
wanted to lash out at Josh for showing me how wrong I had
been to leave him in the first place. I made no mention of
his father.

It was a sincere letter. It was a self-serving letter. I didn't
send it.

Five days after I had left I went back to the studio. An-ling stayed behind her screen. I could hear the tapping of her laptop keys. We said nothing to each other as I packed my belongings. I hadn't brought a lot. I took away even less.

"You have to vacate the loft at the end of June. I'll pay the maintenance until then," I said aloud. I dropped a check on the kitchen counter. A week's pay, enough for a flight to China for the trip she'd always wanted. That was what I wrote in my note. I also wrote, "I'm too angry, too dumb-founded to talk to you, An-ling. All I can say is that I feel betrayed."

At the door I buttoned my raincoat slowly, jangled my keys, waiting for her to peek from behind the screen she had meticulously painted with a scene of filial piety.

Please don't go.

I'm so sorry.

I didn't mean to hurt you.

I'll miss you.

Thank you, Lady Teacher.

She let me leave in silence. As though she had always expected it. As though that was what she wanted.

FIFTEEN

On the witness stand is Inez Serrano, director of the Welcome School where the defendant teaches. She is a handsome woman in her forties with long black hair twisted in an old-fashioned bun at the nape of her neck. She is wearing a black suit and a scowl on the perfect oval of her face.

"When did Mrs. Perotti start teaching Saturday morning classes?" Guzman asks.

"The first week of January of last year."

"She taught from nine a.m. until one p.m., is that correct?"

"Yes."

"Four classes in all?"

"Yes."

"Did you ask her to teach those additional classes?"

"No, she asked for more classes and I offered the Saturday morning slot as the regular teacher was going on maternity leave."

"Did she tell you why she wanted to increase her workload?"

"She said she needed the money."

"I see. Did she ever miss a Saturday class?"

Serrano sucks in air, looks at the defendant.

"Once she called in sick, but she got over it and was in school by nine-thirty."

"Do you remember when that was?"

"No, I didn't remember," she says in an angry tone. "You made me look it up, that's how I remember. It was March twentieth."

"Thank you. A few more questions, Miss Serrano, and your ordeal will be over. On the afternoon of Tuesday, April nineteenth, did you answer the school telephone?"

"Yes. The receptionist was on her lunch break."

"Please tell us about the phone calls you answered?"

"You're only interested in the one for Ms. Perotti."

"Mrs. Perotti received a phone call?"

"I just said that."

"Did the caller identify himself or herself?"

"She said she was An-ling. No last name."

"Do you recall what she said?"

"She wanted to speak to Ms. Perotti." Serrano stresses the Ms.

"What time did the call come in?"

"Just after two p.m."

"How can you be sure of the time?"

"Ms. Perotti's first afternoon class starts at two. She doesn't like interruptions."

"Did you interrupt her?"

"Yes. Miss Huang said it was urgent. She sounded upset."

"Did she tell you anything else?"

"No. I called Ms. Perotti out of her class and she went to take the phone call in her cubicle."

"What happened after that?"

"After a few minutes, I saw Emma, Ms. Perotti, go back to her classroom. After class she came to my office and said something had come up and she had to leave. I told her not to worry, that I would teach her last two classes."

"Did Mrs. Perotti explain why she had to leave?"

"I don't need explanations from Ms. Perotti."

"Did she seem angry?"

"Objection!"

"Overruled."

Serrano takes a moment before answering, seemingly searching for the right words. "She seemed concerned," she finally says.

"Do you know what time Mrs. Perotti left the school?"

"Yes. I accompanied her to the elevator, which is on the way to her class. She took the elevator at ten after three. The next class started at three-fifteen. I did not see her leave the building."

"Thank you. No further questions."

Subj: Fairytales and fantasies
Date: 04-12-05 03:31:54 EST
From: Chinesecanary@BetterLateThanNever.com
To: EPerotti@aol.com

You want to hold everything tight in your hand because you think that way you'll keep it forever.

Amy with her black curly hair and sweet grin. How do I know what she looks like when you have no photos of her in your apartment? Curly black hair, smiling and wearing a yellow sweater with Winnie the Pooh sewn on it or a pink striped outfit with ballooning shorts.

You were going to leave me. I just gave you a reason to go sooner. I made it my call.

The Chinese believe that once you save a person, you're responsible for her for the rest of your life, but we live in America. You saved me for a little while. Thank you. I think for a little while I saved you too.

An-ling

PS. Go to Tom's office. Sit at his desk and open his left-hand filing cabinet. Amy's there. She looked like you.

He has photos and photos of Amy. Filed under D. For Daughter? Dead?

Without pictures will you remember me?

"I won't take up much more of your time, Ms. Serrano," Fishkin says in cross-examination. "I'm sure you're anxious to get back to your work."

Serrano nods.

"You've known Emma Perotti how long?"

"Twelve years in September. I hired her."

"Do you consider her a good teacher?"

Serrano smiles for the first time. "Her students love her and her colleagues respect her, which, believe me, doesn't happen a lot."

"You told the jury that An-ling Huang sounded upset on the phone when she asked for Emma Perotti."

"Yes."

"Can you tell us just how upset?"

Guzman stands with a raised arm. "Objection!"

"Your honor, I'm trying to establish An-ling Huang's state of mind prior to her death. It is paramount to the defense's case."

"I'll allow it," Judge Sanders says and turns to Serrano. "You may answer the question."

"The girl was crying into the phone."

Josh

Over spring break, Dad and I went to Washington, D.C. for a couple of days to see the sights: the war memorials, the Capitol, Abe Lincoln sitting in his chair, the whole bit. It was my first time and it should have been great, but Dad wouldn't let me take my laptop with me. He said he wanted my full attention. I couldn't e-mail An-ling and she wasn't answering any of the messages I left on her cell. I called the loft every day, got Mom sometimes, no answer the rest of the time. I was miserable, but I didn't think anything was wrong.

Saturday morning we were on the New Jersey Turnpike coming home and my cell rang. I looked at Dad. He thinks cells should be banned except for emergencies.

"Josh, please. Let whoever it is leave a message."

I knew it was An-ling. I just knew it.

"This is really important, Dad." I answered.

"I don't want to see you anymore," she said.

She was kidding, I thought. "I don't believe you."

"Look, it was just a hook-up, okay. It's over."

I told her I'd call her back in a few hours.

"Don't. I'm bored with fucking little kids." She hung up.

Now I was roadkill, crow food.

Dad had one eye on the road, one on me. "You okay?"

"Yeah."

"Was that your mother?"

"Max. I gotta go over there to practice a new song." Lies come easy once you start.

I took the subway to Brooklyn, telling myself this wasn't happening to me. An-ling was going to open the door laughing and kiss me and say it was just a joke. If it wasn't a joke? Yell at her, beg her to take me back, shake her until she changed her mind, make love to her. I didn't know what. I had a hundred rats' teeth chomping at my insides and my head felt like the whole Manhattan subway system was running through it at breakneck speed.

I called her as soon as I got out of the subway station to get her to come down and open the door. No one answered. I walked over anyway. I rang the doorbell, banged on the door. She called my cell.

"Go away, little boy. I'm through with you."

I don't know when I smashed the cell against the door. I wasn't aware of doing it until I saw the blood on my hand from where the cracked casing cut it. It wasn't a bad cut, but I pressed my finger hard against it and watched the blood ooze out. It felt good.

I waited for a couple of hours. Long enough for the rats' teeth to stop chewing up my insides and the subways in my head to call it a day. On the way back to Manhattan, I kept my thoughts on how I was going to get my great-grandmother's St. Christopher medal back.

I went over to Max's apartment and cried out every drop of water in my body. He wanted to know what was wrong. I told him Mrs. Ricklin's dog got run over by a car.

Tom

Toward the end of March, leaving school one late afternoon, I spotted An-ling standing on the corner underneath a streetlamp. She was in a clutch of students smoking, drinking soda, eating hot dogs from the vendor on the corner, pretending to belong among them. It was an unusually cold March—most days the temperature stayed in the mid- to high-thirties, with so much rain the reservoirs were overflowing—but she was standing there with her midriff bare, slacks tight enough to show the mound of her groin, over her chest something skimpy that the rain rendered transparent.

"Hi, Mister Professor," she called out. "Hi, Tom."

My chest tightened at the sight of her, but I walked right by. I half expected her to follow me as I climbed down the subway stairs. She was after something; I had no doubt about that, but what precisely that something was escaped me.

Seven, eight times I saw her over a two-week period and as the days passed an idea—more of a premonition, truth be told—began to take hold in my head. Her continued presence outside the college, waiting for me, gave me the feeling that something had gone wrong in her relationship with my wife. I had no rational explanations to back me up, no known factors from which to gauge the situation and yet that is what I believed. I realize now that I was overcome with that most idiotic of sentiments, hope, which overrides all sensible thought.

After seeing An-ling for the third time in a week, I called Inez Serrano, a friend of Emma's and her school director.

After much cajoling on my part, she told me Emma had been sleeping at the school for the past week and a half.

When I saw An-ling outside the college the next time, my chest tightened out of joy, not disgust. I believe I even flashed her a smile, one of triumph, but which she interpreted as a sign of encouragement to move on to her next nefarious step.

SIXTEEN

ASSISTANT DISTRICT ATTORNEY Guzman hands some papers to a court officer, then shifts his glance to Judge Sanders. "Your Honor, at this point I offer printouts of Joshua Howells's e-mails as People's Exhibit Fourteen."

After the exhibit is labeled, the court officer hands the papers to the witness, Jerry Potarski, a large, pony-tailed police computer technician in his mid-twenties.

"Mr. Potraski, do you recognize the printouts now in your possession?"

"Sure do. They're printouts of four e-mails I retrieved from Joshua Howells' laptop computer."

"How did you retrieve them?"

"I found them in the hard drive. They'd been deleted from the e-mail file."

"When were these e-mails sent?"

Potarski looks through the printouts. "The first one is dated April thirteenth of last year, then April fourteenth, then April fifteenth. The last one is from April seventeenth."

"Who were these e-mails addressed to?"

"Chinese canary at hotmail.com."

"Were you able to discover who held the Chinese canary account?"

"An-ling Huang."

"Thank you. No further questions."

Fishkin stands up. "No cross, Your Honor."

Emma

I was back home, feeling like an intruder in the apartment I had shared with Tom and Josh for twelve years. I also felt ashamed and immensely stupid. That morning I had gathered my courage and called Tom to meet me there.

The sleigh bells on the front door jingled. Tom had attached them when we first moved in, to mark our comings and goings. I heard keys being tossed from hand to hand, the sound that had first made me notice Tom as we stood on line for a movie way back, twenty-six years ago. A lean, reserved profile, long sideburns already curling with gray, heavy-framed glasses, a chiseled face, reassuring in its strength.

"My father used to play music by tossing his keys," I told him, standing two people behind him. "*Jailhouse Rock*. My mother would start singing."

Tom laughed, guessing I'd made it up.

Now I rested my head on the back of the sofa and shut my eyes. Footsteps in the hallway came closer. Then a hush. He's on the carpet now, he's seen me. Cold air dropped on my thighs as Tom lifted my coat off my lap. He removed my shoes, pressed his warm hands against my toes. I started to cry. Tom took his hands away.

"Are you planning to stay?" It surprised me how far away his voice sounded, how light in delivery his question was.

I felt a gust of cold air and opened my eyes to flapping curtains. Tom had opened the window. It was snowing, flakes swirling against the wall of the opposite building. A cold, demented April. It had been over two weeks since I had told An-ling I never wanted to see her again. I had screamed my fury at her for the whole building to hear.

My coat was neatly folded over the armchair.

"I've been sleeping at the school." I regretted the words as soon as they were out of my mouth. Tom was going to think I was begging for sympathy.

"Have you left her?" Tom asked.

"I want to come home."

Tom stood immobile across the living room, with my boots in his hands. I always forgot how tall he was. Tree Tom, I used to call him, telling him he was the only tree I wanted to climb. My boots were wet. They were going to stain the carpet.

"Is it over?"

"Yes." I sat up. "An-ling is over. Do you want to know why I've come home?" What would I tell him? That she stole money from me, stayed out all night, did drugs—lies that would satisfy his opinion of her? No, I wasn't going to besmirch her to satisfy my anger or Tom's. The truth belonged to Josh. Only he had the right to tell it. What I could tell my husband was that regardless of what An-ling had done, I was coming home anyway. Would he believe me?

"I've stopped requiring details from you, Emma."

"Aren't you at least curious?"

"You've never been very good at explanations for your actions."

"You're right, Tom. I can't explain them even to myself. If you had called just—" I broke off my sentence. "How is Josh? He cancelled last Sunday, said he had a cold. I miss him."

Tom was looking at me warily.

"I miss him." I repeated.

"He's fine." He went back to examining my shoes through his glasses. Black ankle boots, scuffed and dirty from bad weather. Tom, the family shoe-shine boy. Every Sunday with *The Times'* Help Wanted pages spread on the kitchen floor, Tom polished the family shoes, his, hers, Josh's one pair of Timberlands even though they only got worn a couple of times a year. For Tom it was a Sunday ritual as sacred as Mass used to be for me. His way of making sure we put our best foot forward.

"I want to come back to be with you and Josh."

Tom's gaze stayed on the boots.

"Please."

"I talked it over with him at breakfast this morning," Tom said slowly.

"What did he say?"

"I knew you've been sleeping at the school."

"What did he say?"

"Josh would be happy if you came back."

"He said that?" I so wanted to believe it.

"He expressed it in teenager shorthand. 'Great!' is all he said, but the tone of his voice was sincere."

I felt light with joy. "I owe Josh more than he can know. I owe you. I want to erase my debt for good. Please help me do that, Tom."

He left the room without a word.

"What do *you* want?" I followed him into the bedroom.

Tom reached for a magazine from the pile he kept on his bedside table, used the magazine as a tray to carry my boots. He carefully placed them on the floor of his closet. On Sunday he'll shine them for me, was that what he was telling me? "Talk to me, Tom. Please. Our silence hasn't done us any good at all."

"Please keep our home clean of her." He handed me my old sneakers. "I never want to hear her name. No explanations or excuses to me or Josh about what happened or why." He reached for a strand of my hair, twirled it around his finger.

"You never called, Tom. Why couldn't you say, 'With An-ling or without, I love you. Come home'?"

"Would you have come back?"

"Yes."

His fingers stayed in my hair, but the wisp of softness that had touched his face a moment before disappeared. "As far as we're concerned you never left."

"Half of me never did." I took his face in my hands and kissed him softly.

He closed his eyes. "I'm sorry, Emma."

. . .

A few hours later, I was in the kitchen, getting ready to cook dinner for Tom and Josh. Six months had gone by since I'd been there and I played a game I use with my beginner students: find the differences in two similar pictures. I could spot only three. The old spice jars that I kept lined up on the counter had been removed and not replaced. The African violets under their grow lights were gone. The space above the phone where I always hung the World Wildlife calendar was empty.

I set a large pot of water to boil and waited for Josh to come home, the faint hope I had nursed earlier swallowed by the fear that Tom had gotten it wrong, that Josh would turn away from me.

I heard the refrigerator door open behind me. Josh was there, in the kitchen. For a few seconds I imagined turning around, hugging him, covering his face with kisses, overwhelming him with my feelings. I turned on the stove fan even though the only thing cooking on the stove was water. The whirring sound calmed me.

A lobster crawled out of the paper bag I had set down on the counter. I'd always refused to cook lobster and now the thought of plunging a live animal into boiling water turned my stomach. "We're having lobster Fra Diavolo," I announced, still facing the sink, washing salad. Thanks to the din of the fan, my loudness made me sound resolute instead of afraid. How should I start our new life together? Did you finish your science project? How's Max these days? What about that gig you told me about; did it go well?

I turned to face him. "I've come home, Josh." Under dark lashes, deep hazel eyes that seemed to swell when he smiled; full lips that were so pink when he was a baby that Tom accused me of putting lipstick on them. His hair, fine, dirty blond, straggled below his ears. Cheekbones pushed out of a face that had been chubby until this year. With the emergence of cheekbones he'd added a small gold hoop in his left ear. He was holding himself taller these days, aware of his newfound muscles. He worked out on his home gym every day he had told me when I remarked on the change in his body.

I leaned into him. He was growing too fast and my arms wanted to fold him into me and reassure him that his life was going to be worthwhile despite his mother. "I'm sorry I stayed away so long."

Josh tapped the top of his Coke can—a hand-me-down gesture from Tom that was supposed to stop the soda from gushing out—and dropped his eyes to the lobster making its slow way across the counter. "Lobster Fra Diavolo! Great, my fave!" There was no enthusiasm in his voice. Only awkwardness, maybe embarrassment.

Josh popped the can open. Foam spewed out, dripped to the floor, turning into transparent liquid. "I'll get it," he said.

I bent down before he had a chance and wiped up the soda with a sponge. I straightened myself up by holding his elbow. I could only bring myself to make timid gestures. "We're celebrating you, Josh."

He bobbed his head. The grin leaking onto his face made him look no older than ten. "I can go for that!"

"Josh, Sweetie—"

Josh stepped sideways, out of the reach of my opening arms. "Hey, where does my dinner think he's going?" The lobster had sidled to the edge of the counter and was about to fall over. Josh picked it up, rubbed his finger on a spot above its eyes. "It makes him drowsy. He won't know what hit him." He lifted the lid of the pot and slid the lobster into the boiling water. He grabbed the paper bag on the counter and turned it over. Two more lobsters fell in the pot, the water splashing on his arm.

"Oh, Josh! Let me get some ice to put on that."

"Leave it. It's fine. I can get my own ice if I want."

With my eyes I tried to reach behind that closed, remote face to gauge his feelings, to get an inkling of what he was thinking about An-ling, about my coming back. I gleaned no information.

"Want me to rub your forehead, too?" Josh asked.

"How about adding Mom to that sentence?"

The grin came back, forced this time. "Sure. Mom."

"I guess I could use a little numbing."

I hardly felt his touch on my forehead. Close-up he smelled of cigarettes and sweat. He smelled like a man, a sexual being. I pulled away. He was still so young.

"Did Dad ask you a lot of questions about you? An-ling? I mean about why you're back?" His face turned red.

"I'm back because of you." Which was the truth. I even came to think, in the days that followed, that bringing me back to my son had been An-ling's aim all along. "I missed you." I waited for a reaction.

His eyes look almost transparent in their blankness. "There's no need to tell Dad anything."

"There's nothing to tell," I said, adding a smile for reassurance.

I will protect you always, I thought and remembered a time when I had watched Josh, two years old, playing on the floor of this kitchen. We had just moved back to the city. Josh was stacking wooden blocks with lip-sucking concentration. When the blocks were piled as high as he could get them, he peeked at me from beneath the long dark lashes that he had inherited from my mother. His mouth was clamped shut but I knew he was hiding a smile, a smile that with a quick brush of his hand exploded into laughter as the blocks went flying. I forgot my penance, my vow to God, and scooped up my son, buried my nose in his belly, blew on his navel, tickled him, swung him over my shoulder, laughing my love for him out loud for the first time.

Two days later I took Josh to his first city playground in Riverside Park. He was playing near the jungle gym; I sat on a bench nearby, correcting papers. I don't know how much time passed before I was startled by a small gasp, a rush of many colors crossing my line of vision. I looked up to see a woman kneeling on the concrete by the jungle gym. She bent over, her colorful skirt pooling around her, hiding what I took too long to realize was a child. I stood up, scanned the playground for Josh. He was nowhere.

"Josh!" I ran to the jungle gym.

"He is yours?" the woman asked.

Josh was on the ground, silent, his face gone green, his eyes swollen with pain. "Baby!" I bent down, started to lift him up. He howled and slammed his small hands against my chest.

The femur of his left leg was broken in two places. It took months before he'd let me pick him up again. I never let my love for Josh out of my heart again.

Now my son's worried face was inches away from my own. We were together in our home for the first time in months. I felt like a cripple who, having suddenly found her limbs again, was having trouble getting started.

I love you, Joshua Howells, I told his eyes with mine. Always have. Always will.

Out loud I said, "Rinse out your mouth before Dad comes home."

SEVENTEEN

AYESHA KIRBY'S LONG, gauzy skirt catches on the railing as she slides into the witness chair. She is thin, petite, with hair cropped close to her scalp, chiseled features and a complexion the color of almond skins. After she states her profession—dancer and artist's model—Guzman asks, "On April nineteenth of last year, you went to 313 Lowry Street to model for Tod Curtis, is that correct?"

"You got it."

"Was April nineteenth your first time in that building?"

"No way. I modeled for Tod a hell of a long time. I'm in lots of his paintings."

"Exactly how long did you model for Mr. Curtis?"

"Two sessions a week for seven months."

"In your comings and goings, did you encounter residents or visitors at 313 Lowry?"

"Some."

"Do you see any of the people you encountered sitting in this courtroom?"

Kirby points a long arm at Emma Perotti. "Her."

"The defendant?"

"I seen her a coupla times."

"When did you last see her?"

"My last sitting with Tod."

"Can you pinpoint the day?"

"April nineteenth, last year."

"Can you explain under what circumstances you saw her?"

"What's that supposed to mean?"

Guzman's shoulders tighten as his smile widens. "Where and how did you see the defendant on April nineteenth of last year?"

"She was ringing the doorbell on the fifth floor. Tod lives on six and I always walk up 'cause it's good for my quads."

"Did she see you?"

"She didn't turn around, if that's what you mean. I'm pretty light on my feet."

"But you got a good look at her?"

"I saw her profile. She's got one of those long noses. You can't miss it. I said to myself—Jewish or Italian, one of them two for sure."

"Do you recall what time it was when you saw the defendant ringing the doorbell on the fifth floor?"

"I sure do. Three-fifty p.m."

"How can you pinpoint the time so precisely?"

She grins. "Tod did that. I was twenty minutes late and he was pissin' mad."

In his cross-examination, Fishkin asks Ms. Kirby, "How do you know Emma Perotti was ringing the doorbell instead of, say, just standing in front of the door?"

Kirby leans her torso to one side and gives him a slow, patient look. " 'Cause her finger was glued to the bell, that's how, and what's more I could hear the buzzin' comin' from inside."

Fishkin shakes his head. "I should have thought of that. The buzzing must have been very loud."

"If that's a question, I'll tell you that I don't know how loud it was, but it sure was annoying, you know, like those grasshoppers in the summer that never shut up?"

"Then you heard the buzzing more than once?"

"Sure did. I heard it coming up to her floor and going up to Tod's."

"As you were walking up from the fifth floor to the sixth, you kept hearing the buzzer?"

"Yeah. I just said that."

"Did you hear the door open?"

"No, just the buzzin'. If there was anybody in there, they must have been deaf."

Fishkin's eyes shine. "Thank you, Miss Kirby. No further questions."

Emma

I went back to the loft two days before An-ling died, when I knew she would be at school. I still had the keys. Zhong Kui, the demon slayer, watched me as I walked over to the corner and looked at the still life An-ling had been working on. The canvas was crowded with the objects of her everyday life— cell phone, toothbrush, her laptop, a bra, a box of Tampax, a Chinese takeout carton—painted with bold, sure strokes of brilliant color. I surprised myself with how proud the beauty of her painting made me.

Carefully, I crossed to the other side of the loft, trying to avoid the sound of my own footsteps, aware that I was now an intruder. My mattress was stripped bare and held rolls of linen canvas and a jumble of stretchers and unassembled frames.

In the refrigerator was some sticky rice in its takeout carton, a box of dried apricots, an apple. She'd substituted smoking for food; the place smelled like a giant ashtray.

On the bottom shelf was a bottle of iced tea that only I drank. I picked it up and threw it against the wall. The bottle shattered, spraying tea and shards of glass on the wall, the floor, on me. I was sorry the glass hadn't cut me. My anger would have liked to see blood, especially my own.

I grabbed a broom and a sponge, swept up the glass, wiped the stains from the wall and the floor and fought the urge to continue cleaning, to wash the pile of dishes, the cabinets, the bathroom, scour every inch of the place, as if Clorox could remove sins.

In the bathroom I turned off a leaky faucet. Clothes spilled out of the laundry hamper. I emptied it on the floor, sat down next to the mess, held up her T-shirts, her cargo pants, the pink shirt with the missing button she didn't want me to replace. I smelled the towels for her lavender scent. I smelled for sex. The sheets were clean of semen. The relief that came over me was as liberating as it was absurd.

I folded each item—towels, T-shirts, pink shirt, cargo pants, undies, sheets—with care, pressing out the wrinkles with the palm of my hand, as I had always done. At the doorway I looked back into the room. A mouse met my gaze from behind a dirty glass on the kitchen counter. I reached for the broom. The one time An-ling had sighted a mouse on the stairwell she had screamed to wake the dead, convinced it was the ghost of an evil spirit. Killing this mouse would be my last present to An-ling. I tiptoed forward to the kitchen, smacked the broom on the counter. Once, twice. The mouse was too fast for me.

A few blocks away, in the Ukrainian hardware store, I bought a can of insulation foam. The owner remembered me, offered a series of perfect English sentences as my reward for having given him a grammar book.

I went back to the loft and found the hole next to the water pipe, underneath the sink. I inserted the plastic straw into the nozzle, pushed the straw deep into the hole and pressed. A sizzle of glistening foam, as soft and white as shaving cream, bubbled out, swelled and stiffened, until it looked like a giant viscous wart.

Josh

After I swear on the Bible and sit down, Guzman's face goes so soggy with fake pity I want to puke. And I can't look at Mom or Dad. I just know she's crying and Dad's keeping a stiff upper lip but inside he's got to hate me for shaming us all. Why don't I just tell the jury it was all my fault and get it over with?

Guzman inches closer. I think of a sneaking cat with me the bird. Except his step is loud. There's no need for surprise here. I drop my eyes to his feet.

"Joshua, I know this is difficult. I don't want to make it any harder for you."

Fishkin thinks Guzman's going to go easy on me so the women jurors won't get their backs up. Like I believe any of them.

"I'll only ask you a few questions."

His shoes are black, lace-ups. The shine doesn't hide how old they are.

"Did you ever visit An-ling Huang at the loft your mother had rented for her in Brooklyn?"

"Yes. Next you're going to ask me why. I was curious. I'd never been to Brooklyn before. Or been in an artist's loft."

The Judge leans over, her face and hair both gray. "It's better for you if you confine your answer to the question asked." She has this deep, soothing voice and she smiles as she speaks.

"Did you visit An-ling many times?" Guzman asks.

"Yes."

"How many times approximately?"

I drop my hand on my knee to stop it from jiggling. "I have no idea."

"Can you tell us when you went to see her?" He takes another couple of steps closer. The heels of his shoes hit the floor hard. "When did you visit An-ling at her loft?"

"You want dates?" I make it sound like he's asking the dumbest question.

"That won't be necessary. Was there a particular day you saw her?"

"Saturdays."

"When on Saturday?"

"Mornings." I want him to keep walking. I want to hear the sound of his heels again. Not his voice.

"Was your mother there?"

He thinks he's so clever. If I don't answer he's going to move.

"Please answer the question."

He does move. *Thunk, thunk* go the heels. Now I've got him! I look up. "Mom had classes."

"Did you ever visit An-ling on Sundays?"

"No." Guzman wears elevator shoes. Those heels are at least three inches high. That makes me feel better. I mean he's just this poor vain guy who thinks he's fooling people.

"Did your mother have classes on Sunday?"

Fishkin stands up. He's got to be at least six feet tall. "Objection. Hearsay."

"Sustained."

Guzman tries to look like he doesn't care. "Can you describe your relationship with An-ling Huang?"

"We were buddies."

"What did you do together?"

"We hung out. Talked, laughed, ate junk. What friends do."

"You were friends, nothing more?"

I know what's coming next. Let them kick me in jail for contempt of court. I'm not going to answer.

Guzman goes back to his desk, *thunk, thunk, thunk*, and picks up some papers. *Thunk thunk, thunk*, back to me. He's not fooling anyone.

"I am handing Joshua Howells People's Exhibit Fourteen." He hands me the papers. "Joshua, will you please read the e-mails you sent to An-ling Huang the week before her death out loud to the jury."

I'm not ashamed of what I wrote. I'm not. I only wish it didn't hurt Mom so much. I only wish . . .

"Read out the date and time, too."

I wish I was Harry Potter.

"Please read, Joshua."

Here goes, People's Exhibit Fourteen, one naked kid, guts spilling out. "April 13, 11:37 p.m. 'I don't believe this. What happened? What did I do?'"

"A little louder, please."

I'll shout. Lend me your ears so I can bury my family. "'You've got to tell me. I'm going crazy here.'"

"April 14, 6:47 a.m. 'Why don't you answer me? Am I shit all of a sudden? Mom found out, is that it? She put you up to this? There's got to be a reason. Just give me a reason and I'll leave you alone.'

"April 15, 2:12 a.m. 'You said you loved me, why did you change your mind? Is this a sick joke? Did you meet someone else? No, this is Mom's doing, right? She found out and had a fit, didn't she? That's why you dropped me. Just tell me that. Is it Mom's fault?'

"April 17, 9:29 p.m. 'Dad says you can't reach the moon if you don't stretch your arms. I tried, but I guess I have to accept that my arms are too short. You can keep the St.

Christopher medal if you want. It'll keep you safe. I love you, Josh.' "

I fold my e-mails, hand them back to Guzman. I should stop here, but I can't.

"An-ling was great, okay? She was beautiful inside and out and I loved her but my mother loved her even more than I did." I'm looking at Mom now. She's dry-eyed, but her head's going back and forth like one of those window car dolls. "She'd never hurt An-ling."

An-ling alive, that's what I wish for more than anything.

"No further questions, Your Honor."

"No cross, Your Honor," Fishkin says.

The prosecution's next witness is Linda Franklin, an attractive blonde woman in her early fifties. She is wearing a pale blue suit and a calm, self-confident expression.

"How long have you been teaching at the Manhattan Saxton School?" Guzman asks.

"Twenty-five years."

"What do you teach?"

"For the past eight years I've taught eighth-grade English."

"Do you recognize anyone in this courtroom as one of your students?"

"Yes, Josh, the boy with the white polo shirt."

"Joshua Howells?"

"Yes." She nods at her student, gives him a small encouraging smile.

"Do you recall where you were on April nineteenth of last year?"

"I recall perfectly where I was that day. I, and four other

colleagues, took a busload of students on a field trip to the state capitol."

"Did the trip take up the whole day?"

"And then some. We met at the school at six-thirty a.m. and the bus didn't bring us back from Albany until after eight that night because we got a flat tire on the New York Thruway."

"What students went on the trip?"

"The seventh and eighth graders. Forty-one students in all signed up and came on the trip."

"Was Joshua Howells one of them?"

"Yes, he most definitely was."

Guzman gathers his papers from the podium and smiles. "Thank you, Mrs. Franklin." He walks back to his desk, as a court officer escorts Mrs. Franklin out of the courtroom.

Judge Sanders looks at the clock on the wall, which reads 4:05 p.m., then looks back at Guzman expectantly.

Guzman smiles. "I have no more witnesses, Your Honor. The State rests its case."

EIGHTEEN

THE FIRST WITNESSES for the defense are three teachers and four students from the Welcome School, who testify in favor of Emma Perotti's character. After their testimony, Fishkin calls on Mrs. Hannah Owens of Cleveland, fifty-eight years old, short and plump, with carefully arranged gray hair crowning a plain, round face. She is wearing a new pink pant suit which shows suitcase creases, pink pumps and a cream-colored blouse tied at the neck with a bow.

"Mrs. Owens, did you know An-ling Huang?"

"Not with that name."

"Under what name did you know her?"

"Jean Marie. That's the name Bill, God rest his soul, and I gave her. Jean after Bill's mother, Marie after mine. But Jean is what we called her."

"What was your relationship to her?"

"She was my adopted daughter. An-ling was the name the orphanage gave her, but we wanted her to have a nice American name."

Subj: Fairytales and fantasies
Date: 04-14-05 8:00 EST
From: Chinesecanary@BetterLateThanNever.com
To: EPerotti@aol.com

Let me introduce you to Hannah bandana banana, my adoptive mother.

Let me introduce me to you: Abandoned, adopted and Americanized in Cleveland, Ohio.

Her husband traveled a lot to Beijing on business. He was a solar panel expert. In the States they could only get a black baby. That's what he told me. Water Buffalo Bill, my American baba, with a thick neck and a slow mean look. Yellow was better than black.

They bought me in 1983, when I was eleven months old. Adoptions were still illegal then in China. The government spent money on solar panels, but not on millions of abandoned children left to starve in lice-infested orphanages. We were almost all girls, that's why it didn't matter what became of us. Even now, no Chinese mother is allowed to officially leave her child in an orphanage. It brings shame on the government. If we are lucky, we are left on the steps of a hospital during the night and a good heart will find us quickly and hand us over to an orphanage. If not, the wild dogs or the bandits come and carry us away, the dogs to eat us, the bandits to sell us as slaves.

Hannah and Bill paid for me in hard cash bribes, which Bill said should have made me feel I was worth something. They didn't choose me. No wandering around the orphanage to pick the prettiest, the healthiest, the one who smiles back and wins your heart. Even now when adoption is legal, they don't let you choose. Maybe they're thinking if you want a child, you will love any child. Maybe they're thinking a child is like a sack of rice, the same as another sack of rice.

Bill and Hannah had fifteen minutes to make up their minds. I screamed my head off for the full fifteen, Hannah told me, but they took me anyway. To them, my crying was a sign of good health.

I was given dolls to keep me company, crayons to draw with. I had clean clothes to wear and cookies to eat.

When I was eight years old Hannah had a son. They blessed God every minute for their good fortune. At night, when both mama and baby were asleep, Bill would come to my room and tell me not to be sad, not to be jealous of his son because he, Bill, loved me best. He could do things to me and make me do things to him that made him very happy. Hannah never stopped him.

I became a teenager. Bill's visits didn't stop. I worked hard not to let anger seep out of my body, leave footprints on the floor. I brought home good report cards, cleaned up after myself, ran errands, went to church with them on Sundays. In the effort to keep my emotion secret, in the effort not to slam my fist in their faces, I became a pod without the peas, a clam shell without the flesh. What little of me there was left I kept in the library, between the pages of the books I read about China. Jung Chang, Anchee Min, Amy Tan, Bette Bao Lord, Maxine Hong Kingston and many many others—they spun the stories my mother would have told me, stories to grow on, to tell me who I was, warnings to guide my behavior. The glasses and plates kept slipping even when my hands grew large.

A-I

.   .   .

"Mrs. Owens, were you in touch with your adopted daughter at the time of her death?"

"No, sir. She walked out on us a week before she was supposed to start tenth grade. She was fifteen years old."

"Can you tell us what happened?"

"The Lord knows I would if I had any idea. We gave her everything a child could possibly want, but Jean was difficult right from the get-go. We did our damnedest to please her, but she had no gratitude. Just left a note and off she went. Bill hired a detective to find her—cost us a bundle—but she didn't want to come back and I wasn't about to force her. She had a job, she said she was happy. We told her to call us anytime she needed anything and we never heard from her again."

"You mentioned she was difficult right from the start. Can you tell us how?"

Guzman stands up. "Objection! I don't understand the point of this testimony, Your Honor."

"Overruled," Judge Sanders says. "The point Mr. Fishkin is trying to make is perfectly clear, counselor. Please answer the question, Mrs. Owens."

"How was Jean difficult?" Fishkin repeats softly.

"She broke things all the time and then she'd go hide in a closet like she expected me to hit her. The Lord knows I never did that. Bill neither. I mean, sometimes I lost my patience, but I never laid a hand on her. And she wet her bed until she was twelve years old. Can you believe that?

"She never had any friends. A couple of times I invited some of her schoolmates home, but she would go into her room and refuse to come out."

"Do you know why she didn't want any friends?"

"Once she said she didn't deserve them. Poppycock! Is what I said. She was a silly girl sometimes."

"What happened when Jean was eight years old?"

Mrs. Owens's face lights up. "I had my own kid. My son, Michael John."

"How did Jean react to Michael's birth?"

"She seemed fine until one day I got the scare of my life. She was choking him. I told her, 'If you ever pick up my baby again, Bill's going to whip your behind so you won't sit down for a week!'"

"How did she respond to that?"

"She said she was only hugging him."

"You didn't believe her?"

"Well, no. Michael was crying. Now you're going to think we should have taken Jean to one of those head doctors. Bill and I didn't believe in those people. The social worker at Jean's school wanted to pry into our family life. Shamed me to my bones, she did. We'd done nothing wrong. Our minister offered to see what he could do—we're Lutheran—but Bill told him he'd handle her. I kept a close watch on Michael John and kept on going."

"Were there any other times, before or after the incident with your son, when you were worried about Jean?"

"Oh, yes. After. On a school outing to the lake—she was in seventh grade then—she tried to drown herself. Thank the Lord one of the kids saw her disappear underwater and started hollerin' for help."

"What makes you think Jean did it on purpose, that it wasn't an accident?"

"I asked her, that's what. 'Did you want to die, Jean Marie?' I asked her. 'Is that what you were up to?' She looked up at me real hard, like she was concentrating, fishing for a lie. Then she said, 'Yes. It's nice underwater.'

" 'After all we've done for you, why would you want to do that?' I asked her and I got nothing for an answer." Mrs. Owens clasps her chest with both hands. "That girl broke our hearts."

Subj: Fairytales and fantasies
Date: 04-14-05 11:36 EST
From: Chinesecanary@BetterLateThanNever.com
To: EPerotti@aol.com

I stuffed some clothes and the money I had saved from my allowance into a bag and off I went on a Greyhound toward the setting sun.

San Francisco was supposed to be a rest stop, a place to earn passage money to China to find my real mother. I'd read the Chinese outnumbered the whites and that in some streets I'd be able to pretend I was in mainland China. Except that I was lost. Cantonese, Mandarin and all their variations sounded like strange bird sounds to me. Despite my half-moon eyes and the color of my skin, I was very far from being a real Chinese. I got a job with Madame Chai who owned three successful restaurants. Because I was fluent in English she hired me to wear a tight red silk dress with slits up my thighs and greet the white men who came to eat in her best restaurant, The White Crane. If the patrons cupped my behind, I was to bow my head in modesty but not step aside.

I slept on a futon in the storage room. It was for my own good, Madame Chai reminded me each time she deducted my twenty-five-dollar rent from my weekly pay. If I rented a room from a family I'd end up with a "crack in your vase." I kept my shame to myself.

I earned $3.50 an hour for my twelve-hour day, fifty cents more than the other workers because I had the talent of speaking the language of the "white ghosts."

Madame Chai was as fat as a Buddha, with acrylic nails long enough to belong to an empress. After I'd been working for her a few months, she called me up to her bedroom above the restaurant after the lunch service to practice her English on me. She told me it was useless to go to back to China because if my mother saw me on the street she would walk right by me.

"You mean she wouldn't recognize me?"

"A mama always know her baby, no care how old. It is baby who not know mama. Your mama turn away because she no want her shame on you."

"She gave me up because she didn't have the money to feed me. There's no shame in poverty."

"Maybe no money. Maybe your baba married to woman not your mother. Maybe baba crack her vase and run far. Maybe many things. What is not maybe is you here, in gold mountain. A gift a good spirit give you. Stay. Not anger spirit."

I could have gone to work in an office in the white world and gotten better pay, but Madame Chia was as close as I was going to get to a real Chinese mama. I stayed with her for three years, sleeping on the futon in the storage room, where no one came to visit me. From her I learned how to stiffen my sentences, use simple words, how to sound Chinese. By the time she died I was earning seven dollars an hour and not paying rent, but there was nothing to keep me there. I had saved enough money to come to New York with dreams of becoming an artist. At first I rented a room in Chinatown. Everyone spoke Chinese to me and made me feel like the orphan I was, made me want to be a real Chinese immigrant. I saw a sign from your school on the door of Joe's Dumplings shop on Mott Street. That is why I came to your class. To play make believe. But you were kind and I was not who I said I was and I never came back. I moved out to Long Island City and every day I'd take the subway to Manhattan. I'd wander the city and when I saw Columbia University I liked it. Sitting around the campus I could pretend I was an Ivy League student with parents rich enough to pay the tuition or that I was smart enough to have gotten a scholarship there. I could pretend and not have to answer any questions.

From Madame Chai I also learned that the success of a crop depends on three harmonies: the season, the ground, the effort humans make. For a while you and I had a nice crop—many peonies, the flowers of love, affection, feminine beauty, good fortune. It was the human part that failed in the end. Both our efforts. My neediness. Your anger. I'm not the only one to blame.

Your friend, An-ling

Tom

A few days after Emma came home a package arrived in my office with no return address. Inside the jiffy envelope was a small painting of a boy's naked torso, a St. Christopher medal dangling from his fingers. I reached for the scissors, carefully cut the canvas from its frame, and then proceeded to reduce that disgusting painting to small squares no larger than my thumbnail. The poem that had accompanied it I flushed down the toilet.

After I was done I called Emma and told her I wanted to take her and Josh out to dinner. The Terrace, I suggested. "I want to celebrate us. You, Josh, me. Our family. Why not, the bad weather too." We both managed a laugh.

I walked home that afternoon, from 68th Street and Lexington to 112th Street and Riverside Drive. A long leisurely walk on an unseasonably cold day, the first dry day in weeks. Along the way I came across many useful garbage cans.

Subj: Fairytales and fantasies
Date: 04-17-05 19:11.29 EST
From: Chinesecanary@BetterLateThanNever.com
To: EPerotti@aol.com

I sent Josh away in a bad way so he will hate me. Hate builds strong walls. That's my one good deed. My goodbye present.

I read in a Chinese book that a mother will sew her absent daughter a coat and wander the countryside to try and catch her spirit. I like to think my mother did that, but I was too far away for her to find me.

My spirit made a home in your heart for a few months. It was the first time my spirit rested. Thank you for that. Don't be too angry with me. I am not your real family. I am not Amy. I am me. Just me. You weren't going to stay. I couldn't keep you

A-lH :-) :-(:-) :-(:-) :-(:-) :-(:-) :-(:-) :-(:-) :-(:-) :-(:-) :-(:-) :-(:-) :-(:-) :-(:-) :-(:-) :-(:-)

P.S. Thank you for the can of insulation foam. I will make art with it.

Tom

"Did you go see An-ling?" Josh asked this morning.

"Why would I have done that?"

"Weren't you curious?"

There was a sharpness to his voice. I turned to assess his expression—we were eating breakfast side by side, ready for another day in court, waiting for Emma to finish dressing. I perceived his expression as one of fear. It could be nothing else under the circumstances. The trial is winding down. It's Emma's turn to testify today, the defense's last witness.

"Mom will do just fine," I said.

"Did you go see An-ling?" The sharpness turned into a whine.

"Is curiosity what took you there the first time?" I asked.

Josh looked suddenly abashed. I regretted my unfairness, but couldn't bring myself to show it.

"You can tell me, Dad. You went over there, didn't you?"

I took time to answer. His suspicion caught me off guard. "No, Josh, I did not."

"I don't believe you." A rash of anger spread over his face.

"What makes you think I went? Is it something your mother said?" What was he after?

Josh shook his head, his jaw at an unbecoming stubborn angle.

"An-ling?"

"I just know," he said. "You went that last day, didn't you? Didn't you, Dad?" His eyes brimmed with tears and my irritation turned to pity. But how much do you tell a son who is not yet sixteen and whose mother is on trial for murder of the girl who seduced him, the girl whom he probably thinks will be his only great love?

"I didn't go," I told him. "But that doesn't mean that I didn't miss Mom every day. That I didn't want her back. It doesn't mean—"

"I know." Josh knuckled his eyes dry. "It doesn't mean you don't love Mom."

"That's right."

Josh tugged at my arm. "Tell them, Dad. Tell them you went over there that afternoon." His voice was filled with a little boy's passion. "You didn't mean to hurt her, but you were really angry and it just happened. Tell them, Dad. Please."

I shook him hard. "What are you saying?" He just stared, eyes wide. I'd never hurt him before. "What are you thinking?"

He squirmed out of my hands. "They won't believe you. There's no evidence against you, and you're her husband. You're lying to save Mom, that's what they'll think, but they'll have to let her go. It's reasonable doubt. You won't go to jail. Dad, get her off!"

I took my son in my arms and held him tight. "What a good son you are. We're so lucky to have you." My beautiful son. I love him so much. "Everything is going to be fine, Josh. I promise. Fishkin is confident. So am I." I let go but left my arm around his shoulder. My son, the ballast of my life.

"You know what I kept remembering during the months your mother was away? I kept remembering the moment I decided I wanted her to be my wife. We were on the

Observation Deck at the World Trade Center, our first time up there. The sky was clear and the view was neverending. Your mother was rapt. I watched her face reflected in the window. She looked so tender, so small, like a little girl, and then she turned to me and she was this beautiful woman and then for a minute there I saw the lovely old woman she would become. That's when I knew I wasn't going to let her go. She was going to be part of my life for as long as there was breath in me."

"The towers are gone; the world's flipped out and nothing is ever going to be good again." Josh stepped out of my reach. "Tell them you were there, Dad."

After everything that had happened, I wasn't going to lose him now. "All right, I'll talk to Fishkin. If he thinks it's a good idea, I'll do it."

"What's a good idea?" Emma asked as she walked into the kitchen, offering us a nervous, subdued smile.

My beautiful wife. She has never blamed me for Amy's death. I knew Amy could open the front door. I'd seen her do it just days before she died. I'd even complimented her. "What a clever little girl you are," I'd said. Penn State football was on TV when Amy ran out to the street. My alma mater, my team. That's what was on my mind when it happened. I never told Emma. Amy's death is my fault.

"It's a good idea to get going," I said. "We've got a big day ahead of us."

"I'm ready," she said. Josh linked his arm in hers, walked her down the corridor to the front door, mother and son together.

Guilt is a weight that should grow lighter with the years. I expected it to become a memory, its edges softening with time, the middle blurring until it thinned to a slim disk, conveniently movable out of sight. I never imagined it would finally tear through me.

"Hey, wait up you two."

NINETEEN

THE DEFENDANT, EMMA Perotti, is on the stand. She is a tall, soft-bodied fifty-two-year-old, with short graying hair, an oval unmade-up face and wide heavy-lidded brown eyes. A writer for an upscale women's magazine has described her as having the flat look of an Alex Katz portrait. The sketch artists in the courtroom find her likeness hard to capture.

Emma

My lawyer walks to the podium, gives me a small nod of encouragement. "Good morning, Ms. Perotti." He has convinced me to tell the truth, not to be afraid to bare my soul to these strangers. They sit in judgment of every breath I take. How can they possibly understand?

I will keep my eyes on Fishkin's face, a kind one. I take a deep breath. "Good morning," I say.

"Please tell the court in your own words what happened on April nineteenth of last year, the day the woman you knew as An-ling Huang died."

"She called me at school in the afternoon. Inez, Ms. Serrano, called me away from the class. I hadn't talked to An-ling since I'd left the loft. Almost three weeks, I think it was. She said, 'I need to see you.' "

Her voice was high-pitched, splintered by sobs.

"Are you all right?" I said.

"Yes, I'm happy, awesomely happy, totally happy. Your check's in my pocket, my bags are packed and I'm going so far from you; you'll never catch my spirit. But first I want to say goodbye, leave you the key, show you that I haven't painted FUCK OFF all over the walls. I've even vacuumed. I want you to be proud of me. I'm leaving you all my paintings, the screen too. Maybe you can get some money for them for the rent."

"That isn't necessary."

"That was our deal, remember?"

"I would have preferred loyalty," I told her.

I tell the jury, "She asked me to come over. She said she was going away and wanted to say goodbye in person."

"Did she sound upset?"

"Yes. She was crying."

"Why didn't you go right away?" Fishkin asks.

"I had classes to teach. And then I was still angry with her because of my son. I didn't realize how desperate she was."

. . .

"You have to come over." Her tone was that of the child who wants, who can only envision the now.

I wasn't going to let her maneuver me like that. "Leave the keys on the table then and thank you for cleaning up. That was sweet and I appreciate it. I do. Please send me a note when you get to China and let me know you're well." If I could sell her paintings I'd send her the money. "Be well, An-ling, and be safe."

"Please come," she repeated.

"What did you tell her?" Fishkin asks.

"I told her I'd be there after my classes, around five o'clock, but then I got worried. She had sounded so unhappy. I asked Ms. Serrano to take over and went to the loft. When I got there, I rang the doorbell for the longest time."

"Didn't you still have keys to the loft?"

"Yes, that's how I let myself in downstairs, after ringing the bell to let her know I was on the way up. I didn't want to barge into the loft. I no longer lived there. After ringing the doorbell for maybe three to five minutes, I assumed she'd left and I used my key."

"What did you find when you walked in?"

"She was dead." Her body twisted on the floor, her mouth wide with hardened foam. I lifted her up against my chest. From the floor underneath her, Josh's medal and broken chain glimmered at me. I snatched them up, stuffed them in my pocket, and then I rocked her, sang to her, recited poems we had read together. In the hospital they had taken Amy away from me.

"I held her for a long time." It was dark when I heard a burst of trumpets. Tod Curtis, the upstairs tenant, blasting his classical music for the entire neighborhood to hear. I became aware of the outside world again. After him, maybe others would come. I removed the robe An-ling was wearing and eased her back on the floor. I got up and went to strip the sheet from her futon. The sheet and the cover, the towels in the bathroom, the sponge in the sink, anything that my son could have touched, I threw in the washing machine. Then I kneeled down next to An-ling and washed her face with soap to remove her makeup, to make her look like the young sweet girl she really was. I dragged the futon next to her, put a clean sheet on it and, lifting up first her torso, then her legs, slipped her onto the futon.

"I held An-ling until my arms hurt. When she started to stiffen I lay her back on a clean sheet on her futon. I crossed her arms over her chest and kissed the top of her head, covered her with another sheet." The same ritual I had performed after discovering Nonna dead on her bed. "I pulled the screen in front of the bed and opened it fully. It was my burial ceremony."

"When you found your son's medal and chain under An-ling's body, did you think he had killed her?"

"I panicked and forgot he was safe in Albany. Forgot his gentleness, his goodness. He would never have killed her. Never. I just lost my mind." Tears come unexpectedly, pour down my face, drip from my chin. I shake my head to gain control. Fishkin hands me a handkerchief.

"What did you do after your burial ceremony?"

"I tried to remove all traces of my son's relationship with An-ling." I looked for the portrait of Josh's naked body. I didn't find it. Either Josh had it or she had done me a favor, destroyed it. Then I did what even a bad mother would do.

"I cleaned the can of his possible fingerprints. I was too focused on Josh to realize what a wiped-clean death weapon would mean to the police." When I left I walked to the East River and dropped Josh's medal, chain and An-ling's laptop in the water. From a nearby phone booth I made an anonymous call to the police.

"Emma, you are under oath." Fishkin says. "You have sworn to tell the truth."

"Yes."

"Did you kill the woman you knew as An-ling Huang?"

It is time to face them. I turn and look at the twelve men and women who will decide if I am innocent. Their faces are impassive except for one droopy-eyed black woman. She leans forward on her seat and studies me with a look full of concern. "No, I did not kill An-ling," I tell her.

I form a picture in my mind of Amy and An-ling together, two sisters perched on the sun, gleefully throwing needles down to earth. The image eases my guard, allows me to speak from the heart.

"I am guilty only of letting my own feelings, my self-absorption, make me forget how unhappy, how fragile An-ling was. An-ling killed herself—I have no doubt about that—and I take some of the blame. For being too harsh with her, for giving her the illusion that I would always be there for her, no matter what she did. I abandoned her.

"I will always carry the thought that if I had gone to the studio earlier, she would be alive today. Every day I picture myself consoling her, making peace with her, reassuring her that she isn't a throwaway girl. I hear myself tell her that I will always help, always be her friend.

"Never, not even when I was very angry with her, did I want anything bad to happen to An-ling. Please believe me, I did not push the nozzle of that can."

Josh

Dad said Fishkin nixed my idea about him confessing to killing An-ling as being too obvious. The judge wasn't going to buy it and it would destroy Fishkin's defense: that An-ling killed herself. Four days ago, Guzman spent the whole day cross-examining Mom. He was mean, but she didn't crack. No tears this time. When he asked her, "Why did you leave your family to live with An-ling Huang?" she answered, "My family is privileged. An-ling was not. I thought I could help her. I never meant to stay as long as I did." She didn't bring up Dad, their fights.

"You didn't think your son needed your help?"

She looked at me, her face getting real soft, blurry. I knew she was trying to tell me how sorry she was. I knew then she really loved me. All I could think of was giving her a thumbs-up sign.

"I'd seen the scars on An-ling's wrists," Mom said. "An-ling, from what I knew at the time, had no one."

The next day we got the lawyers' closing statements. Fishkin went first and said the evidence showed that Mom was a generous and kind person who tried to help a desperately unhappy artist. The evidence showed she loved me very much because she destroyed any evidence that might connect me with An-ling's death.

Then Guzman got up and said the evidence showed without a reasonable doubt that Mom cared only about An-ling and when she found out about me making love to her, she got so jealous and angry she killed her.

Which evidence was the jury going to believe? And what was I going to do with the evidence playing in my head?

It's been two and a half days. Fishkin says the longer it takes, the better it is for Mom. Worms are eating up my stomach; that's what it feels like.

The judge walks in and we all stand up. The court officer hands him a note. That could mean the jury has reached a verdict. Mom turns to look at me and Dad and smiles, like she knows it's going to be okay.

An-ling's last e-mail, the one Mom never saw, the one I burned—she wrote it her last day, at 2:37 p.m, after she called Mom, before she tried to get me:

Tom's coming over. I didn't tell you on the phone because you wouldn't believe me. It's true. I'm going to tell him I know he's kept Amy's photos hidden from you. I'm going to tell him he's the one who killed Amy.

You, Lady Teacher, are only guilty of thinking a dog's life is important. Maybe Tom will want to hit me and maybe he'll want to do other things too. Like Bill used to.

I left the door open downstairs. I know you're already on your way. Hurry. I'll hide you behind a screen. With you here, Tom won't scare me. You'll stop him from hurting me.

A-l

Why do I believe her? She lied so much. And even if—Shit, the jury's coming through the door.

An-ling, please help Mom. Amy. God. Please!

Tom

What I could have told my son:

Tuesday, April 19, the temperature in the mid-forties— still coat and glove weather. Thankfully no rain. I had initiated the call to An-ling after another letter of hers had arrived at my office. She had expected a visit, she said. I rose to her bait willingly. I even looked forward to our meeting. There is nothing that gives more satisfaction than the conviction that you have found the solution to a stomach-churning problem.

She had left the door of the building open. I walked up, saw no one. She was waiting for me at the door of the apartment. "You want to get rid of that?" she asked, pointing to my Burberry. I shook my head. I didn't want anything of

mine to touch anything of hers. I was wearing gloves for
that purpose.

"I'm happy you came." She closed the door behind me
and with her free hand tried to lead me inside. I lifted my
arm out of her reach. I had no intention of going any further than just inside that closed door. Against one wall was
a large canvas, blank except for a long bloated squiggle of
what I now understand was insulation foam. The can stood
on the floor, straw attached.

"Do you want tea? That's all I've got."

I shook my head again. She didn't deserve the civility of
words. The studio was overheated, the air stale with smoke.
She was wearing thick make-up: red lipstick, a line of deep
green on each eyelid. Two slashes of pink on her cheeks. She
looked ludicrous. I was sure that underneath her short silky
bathrobe she was naked. She had seduced my wife, then my
son and now I was to be her third conquest.

"Nothing I can get you?" As she spoke, she let herself fall
against my chest. I watched, as you might watch an exotic
creature behind a cage, as her face slowly tilted up toward
mine. Her tongue reached my chin, licked it. Her body was
light, soft; she smelled of candy. In the heat of that room I
turned hard and lost myself. I grasped her buttocks, lifted
her up to my waist. She pressed against me, her thigh heavy
on my hips and moaned, "Tom." A wet animal sound. Barely
recognizable. And yet, my name. Tom.

She dropped down, pushed me away. Her eyes gleamed
and I got the feeling that what was occurring between us
was all according to her plan.

"What the fuck do you want?" I said.

She thrust her shoulders back, exposing the white of her chest. I thought it was part of her pitiful seduction routine, but what she was showing me was the medal hanging from her neck.

She turned the medal and held it up with one hand. I leaned closer and pretended to read the name I already knew was there: *Celestina Fenoli*, Emma's grandmother. I snapped the chain from her neck.

"You're the one who killed Amy," she said. "You were supposed to watch her, Tom. It wasn't Emma's fault." I struck her. As I raised my arm again, she jumped back, tripped on the can and fell to the floor, hitting the back of her head with a sharp smack. She lay there, eyes closed, the can rolling to my feet.

I left her on the floor.

My gloves ended up in a trash can in Brooklyn, my Burberry in a construction dumpster on my way to Hunter. I thought that Josh's medal and chain were in one of the pockets. I was ridding myself and my family of her. She was a cheap little whore who was trying to destroy my family. Now, after what I've learned at the trial, I realize she was a sick girl like so many who are free to walk the streets. Their twisted minds aren't recognizable until it's too late and they crash a brick on some innocent bystander's head or shove someone into an oncoming subway train.

The jury is filing back into the courtroom. I have never doubted what the verdict would be, which is why I have kept silent about my visit to An-ling. No jury would believe I left the girl alive. I had to stay out of it for Josh's sake. He still needs me. They both need me.

. . .

The jury files into the room. After the seven women and five men take their places, Judge Sanders says, "You have sent me a note saying you have reached a verdict. Is that correct?"

The foreman stands. "Yes, Your Honor."

"Please answer the court clerk."

The court clerk, a thin balding man who has been sitting behind a desk to one side of the courtroom, reading his newspaper for most of the trail, now stands up and reads from a sheet of paper.

"To the charge of murder in the second degree, how—"

The juror sitting next to the foreman, a black woman with big drooping eyes, cannot wait. She turns to look at the defendant's son, Joshua Howells, and lifts her cheeks in a wide, victorious smile.

TWENTY

Emma

JOSH WANTED TO celebrate the Not Guilty verdict with prayer. He tried to convince Tom to come too, but Tom, the unbeliever, said it was a good time for Josh and me to share each other's company without his presence. I chose Saint Patrick's, the place of a promise made, a promise that needed to be unmade.

"We don't have a picture of her, Mom." We're sitting in the front pew. "In that message she left," Josh tugs at his ear, Tom's gesture when he's weighing his words, "she said, 'Don't erase me, Drummer Boy. Let me stay with you.'

"She had that funny mouth, remember?" Another tug. I skate my hand down his back. "No dip in the middle. And that thick hair and . . . oh, God!" He throws himself back against the pew, his face scrunched with disbelief. "I'm already forgetting what she looked like."

"Do you remember how she made you feel?"

He nods as a blush blooms over his cheeks.

"That's what she'd want you to hold on to."

There are only a few people praying. Tourists walk the aisles, pointing, whispering. Feet scuffle. Camera flashes burst from darkened corners. In front of the side chapels, hundreds of candles flicker orange light.

"You think God's here?" Josh asks after a long stare at the crucifix above the high altar.

"Here, there, wherever you want God to be if you believe."

"I'd like to believe. I think I do now, after—" he shrugs. "I mean, it's easier. It's not all up to me."

"Yes, it's easier."

"During the trial I tried praying, coming to church. You used to do that, right? Before Amy died?"

"Yes."

"Do you think An-ling believed in God?"

I wrap my arm in his. "I don't know. She believed in the old traditions of her country. That's a religion of sorts."

"Why did she lie so much, Mom?"

"She was trying to be someone else and she wanted love from everyone."

"She lied a lot."

"Don't hold it against her, Josh. She couldn't help herself. Think of how unhappy she was."

"No, I'm glad she lied. It means—" Josh lowers his head.

"It means what?"

Josh doesn't answer. His lips start to move and I keep his arm wrapped around my own as he prays.

When he raises his head I say, "The last time I came here I was pregnant with you. I asked God to take care of you and keep you safe. In exchange I promised I would not allow myself the joy of loving you openly. It was a very stupid thing I did. It's nothing God would have wanted. I always have loved you, Josh."

"I know."

"Please forgive me."

"Forget it, Mom. That's old stuff."

"Please forgive me for everything."

He nods. "Me too?"

"You were only being young."

He blushes again. "You should get to know Max's mom. All she thinks about is her committees. Max has to do his own laundry."

That thought makes me smile. "You'd go naked before that happened."

He leans over and kisses my cheek. "You got it." I kiss him back and we sit there for a long time, arms linked, letting the grace of the cathedral lull us into a state of peace.

The verdict has not wiped my conscience clean or taken away my sadness over An-ling's death, but I can't help also being happy. I've been given another chance to make amends. To become the woman I once set out to be. To watch my son grow into a man.

The pew creaks when we finally stand up. I follow Josh down the center aisle. He stops abruptly next to the last pew where a man sits hunched, head buried in his arms.

I recognize Tom's windbreaker. "Tom?" His shoulders start to shake.

"I'll wait outside," Josh says.

I take hold of his hand. "Please stay."

He walks to the other end of the pew. We slide in, one on each side of Tom. I embrace him. Josh pats his back. Tom's sobs grow loud.

His depth of visible emotion is unusual, surprising; it frightens me. "What is it, Tom?" I whisper, kiss his neck.

"God, I'm so sorry," Tom cries into his arms. "I didn't mean—"

"Shh, it's okay." I think I understand now. "It's all right, Tom. Amy's in the past. We're only going to think of Josh now." I caress his head with my hand, over and over, in an effort to quiet him. "Our beautiful boy."

Tom hugs me. His chest trembles against mine. Maybe he is also crying for the marriage we almost destroyed. Our lives as a couple and as individuals are weighted with a great deal of unhappiness, missteps, selfishness, but we can try to fight for pockets of serenity. I am determined to fight, for myself, for Tom, especially for Josh. As a family we must stitch the holes in our lives back together with solid thread. As a family we have to make sure that Josh's future, our future, has light in it. That is my hope, my goal. If it is not too late.

I rock my husband turned into a child. "It's over, Sweetie."

"Come on, Dad." Josh stands up, tugs at his father's sleeve. Tom stays hunkered down in my arms. "You said everything was going to be fine. You promised, remember?" Josh sits back down and hugs Tom from behind. "I love you, Dad."

Tom's tears take a long time to stop and when they do we sit in silence, each lost in our own hopes and prayers until Josh says, "Come on, guys. Let's go."

The sudden sun outside the cathedral is blinding. Blinking, we turn in the direction of home.

Josh

Grams liked to say that no tree throws a shadow as long as the past, but that's only if you let it. Mom let Amy's death get to her all those years and Dad did his crying when no one was looking and I guess An-ling never got over all the bad stuff that happened to her. I'm not going there.

Maybe An-ling made up that last e-mail or maybe Dad did go over to the loft that afternoon. If he did, he probably yelled his head off at her and made her feel terrible, and she killed herself after he left. There are many ways of looking at this thing.

Whatever he did, if anything, he did it for my sake and Mom's. We're all he's ever worried about.

I go to church sometimes now. Mom comes with me. I'm working on Dad.

I've told the priest all about us, Amy and An-ling. He says that whatever really happened, what's important is to feel remorse and to remember the need to forgive, to be forgiven.

I'm trying to do that.

He said that tragedies can divide or unite. In my family we've had ones that did both. It's up to us which way it goes now.

Mom and I light candles to Amy and An-ling whenever we're in church. I told Dad you don't have to believe in God to do that. It's just a way of remembering them. That's what they'd want. For us never to forget.

Acknowledgments

Many helped me shape this novel: Marie Damon, Ann Darby, Barry Greenspon and the staff of The Drummer's World, John Grossman, Jane Grossman, Jennifer Gundlach, Judith Keller, Robert Knightly, Dr. Barbara Lane, Maria Nella Masullo, Joan Meisel, Annette and Martin Meyers, Willa Morris, Judy Moskowitz, Geoffrey Picket, Sue Richman, Linda Sicher, Marilyn Wallace and Susan Wallach. I thank them for their expertise, their editorial skills, their patience, and most of all their friendship. I especially thank my editor, Katie Herman, for her keen eye and my publicist, Sarah Reidy, for her unrelenting enthusiasm. If there are mistakes, they are my own.

To Stuart—my gratitude and love.